DANGEROUS BEAT

CHARLOTTE FLYNN

AN ARCHWAY PAPERBACK
Published by POCKET BOOKS • NEW YORK

AN ARCHWAY PAPERBACK *Original*

An Archway Paperback published by
POCKET BOOKS, a division of Simon & Schuster, Inc.
1230 Avenue of the Americas, New York, N.Y. 10020

ISBN: 0-671-50783-4

First Archway Paperback printing May, 1985

10 9 8 7 6 5 4 3 2

AN ARCHWAY PAPERBACK and colophon are
registered trademarks of Simon & Schuster, Inc.

MOONSTONE is a trademark of Cloverdale Press.

Printed in the U.S.A.

IL 5+

DANGEROUS
BEAT

Chapter 1

"Okay, Lois Lane, go get 'em," Jennifer's father called out to her as she climbed into the little silver Datsun. Jennifer waved out the window at him, squinting into the bright morning sun. She backed onto Webster Avenue, looking at the rear window to be sure she didn't thump into Mr. Ander's station wagon parked at the curb. On the first day of her new job at the *Springfield Times*, she didn't want to be part of a story about a fender-bender.

Jennifer guided the car along tree-lined Webster Avenue to the Roosevelt Expressway, which would take her downtown. It had been a wonderful last-minute surprise when her father had given her the keys to the family's second car, which her mother usually drove. "It's time your mother got a new car, anyway," he'd said. "Besides, now that you're a reporter, you'll need wheels. It's yours for the summer."

"Well, I'm not a reporter just yet," Jennifer had reminded him.

"All right," he had laughed, "a summer copygirl needs wheels, too." Of course, she hadn't argued with him. Having her own car to use was almost as terrific as having a job on Springfield's number-one newspaper.

Jennifer pulled onto the expressway and drove slowly in the morning rush-hour traffic. In the distance she could just make out the skyline of Springfield along the river.

To everyone else it was just another workday, but to Jennifer it was a dream come true. She'd worked on the school newspaper, the *Clarion*, for a few years, but this was the real thing. At last she'd be helping to put out a professional paper. Up until two months earlier, that had seemed an impossible goal.

She thought back to the day when Tom Whitney, the entertainment editor of the *Times*, had come to Jefferson High to talk to the *Clarion* staff. He had looked so distinguished. Tall, slim, dressed in a blue suit with a conservative striped tie, and wearing horn-rimmed glasses, he had given Jennifer the impression that his eyes penetrated right into her. But even though he was an important newspaper editor, when he started talking with the *Clarion* staff, he was open and friendly, treating them like equals, chatting with them as one newsperson to another. Soon he'd taken off his jacket and rolled up the sleeves of his blue shirt, and as she listened to him, she realized that despite his relaxed attitude, Tom Whitney was very serious about his

2

profession. Studying people, trying to figure out what they were really like inside and why they acted the way they did, was something Jennifer found interesting. It was one of the reasons she wanted to be a reporter.

And now I'll actually be working with Tom Whitney, Jennifer thought as she drove toward the *Times* building. She remembered exactly how she had lucked into the job. Someone on the *Clarion* staff had asked Tom what made a good story.

Tom had picked up the current edition of the *Clarion* and held it up. "Here's a good story, right here in your own school paper," he had said. He had looked at the author's by-line on the story. "Who's Jennifer Taggert?" Jennifer had blushed and raised her hand. "Nice story," he had said. "Clear, concise, all the information included."

That had given her the courage to go up to him after his talk and ask if there was any possibility of her getting a summer job on the paper. He had smiled. "I can't promise you anything, but why don't you drop around the *Times* office one day and we'll have a chat."

She had stopped by the very next day and that was how she won a summer job as a copyperson. She felt very fortunate to be able to work at the *Times* while still a seventeen-year-old high school senior. Writing was her passion, and she wanted nothing more than to be a professional reporter. And now she would find out exactly what it meant to work on a real metropolitan daily paper.

Leaving the expressway, she drove over to Manchester Avenue, then entered the employees' parking lot behind the gray stone *Times* building. She passed the parking spaces reserved for the high-ranking editors and slid the Datsun into a space near the end of the lot away from the building.

She walked quickly across the parking lot, excitement beating in her heart, and went up the sweeping stone steps of the building. The security guard eyed her curiously. Jennifer reached into her bag for the lime-green *Springfield Times* press card she had been issued. The guard gave it a quick look and grinned. "I'm Danny," he said. "Nice to have you working with us, Jenny."

Jennifer smiled warmly and headed for the elevator. She had been told to report to Mike Monrony, the city news editor, on the seventh floor, but she decided on a final personal inspection before she met him. In the rest room, she checked herself in the mirror, critically examining her appearance. The reflected image was that of an intelligent, attractive young woman with shiny dark hair, alert brown eyes, and a lovely slim figure. Jennifer had carefully chosen her outfit, a flared maroon plaid skirt and a short-sleeved white blouse. It made her look like a professional. She pulled a brush out of her bag and ran it through her hair a few times. She reapplied her lip gloss, which she'd chewed off in her nervousness. "Well, I guess I'm as ready as I'll ever be," she said to the image in the mirror and walked briskly into the hallway.

She passed the reception desk and a sign reading

"Editorial." Then she went along a short corridor and into the enormous city news room, the heart of the *Springfield Times*. She had seen it briefly once before, the day Tom Whitney had hired her. But on that occasion her usual powers of observation had temporarily deserted her in the excitement. Now she took a better look.

The city news room was a vast, squared space, packed with the desks of reporters and editors, many with video display terminals, used for writing stories. Men and women typed frantically and dashed to and fro clutching papers. Everywhere was a flurry of activity. Hanging from the ceiling in the center was a large, four-sided clock that was visible from every part of the big room. It was a constant reminder to the *Times* staff that a deadline was coming, had arrived, or was already past.

Jennifer recognized the city news editor at his desk. Mike Monrony was hunched forward, talking intently on the telephone. He had a cigar in his mouth that he chewed as he talked. She went slowly over to him and waited until he had finished his conversation. He hung up the phone and glanced inquisitively up at her.

"Yes?"

"Hello, I'm Jennifer Taggert," she said.

Mike Monrony smiled broadly and stood up. He was slightly beefy, with a wild mop of blond hair. He spoke and moved quickly, something Jennifer had noticed in a number of newspaper people. She guessed that was because they were always conscious of time. "Well, hello, Jennifer," he said, extending a slightly damp

5

hand. "Welcome aboard. You're the kid from the *Clarion,* aren't you?"

"Yes, sir," she said, shaking his hand firmly.

Monrony relighted his dead cigar. "Let me give you the first rule of a newspaper. I'm Mike, not 'sir.' We're all more or less equal around here." He grinned. "Of course, some of us are more equal than others." He laughed shortly.

"Okay . . . Mike," she said, feeling a blush rising to her face at using his first name so casually.

That kind of informality was what Jennifer loved about the news business. The paper needed lowly copygirls as much as it needed top editors. It was the same feeling of equality she had sensed when she first met Tom Whitney.

"Jack," Monrony called to a small, older man who sat across from him, "meet our new copygirl, Jennifer Taggert."

"Hi, Jenny," said the man.

"Jenny, this is Jack Markman, the assistant city news editor. He'll tell you what to do. Good luck." And Mike quickly grabbed his phone, already ringing again, and started talking away at top speed.

"Well, Jennifer," Jack said hurriedly, apparently in even more of a rush than his boss, "has anyone filled you in on the duties of a copyperson?"

"No, sir," she said politely.

"Call me Jack," he said quickly. "You see that bench over by the door?" Jennifer glanced across the room to a long wooden bench, where several young people sat watching the room attentively. "Well, a copyperson sits on that bench. And when someone yells out 'copy,' that means they want something. Whatever they want, you get it. Usually, it's coffee." He smiled. "Now I assume Tom Whitney showed you around the building when he hired you, so you'll know generally where things are when you're sent on an errand. If you're not sure, just ask someone. We're all happy to help."

"All right, Jack," she said. "Thanks for your time. I'll let you go back to your work." She walked briskly across the room to the copypersons' bench.

Her first job was to bring some page proofs to Tom Whitney in the entertainment department. That was lucky because she knew exactly where to go. She found Tom's tiny office in a corner of the entertainment room, and he smiled genially as she hurried in. She handed him the ink-stained page proofs, which were copies of that day's entertainment section exactly as they would appear in the *Times*.

"On the job, I see," said Tom, taking the pages. He leaned back and pushed his horn-rimmed glasses back onto the bridge of his nose. "How's it going?"

"All right," she said. "Everybody sure is busy."

Tom laughed. "Oh, yes. Things happen in a hurry around here."

He stood up and walked Jennifer out of his office. He waved to a woman at a desk across the small room. "Kathleen, this is Jennifer, a new copygirl. Jenny, Kathleen Owens, our resident music critic."

Kathleen rose from her desk and shook Jennifer's hand. "Hello, Jennifer," she said softly.

7

Kathleen was tall and slim in a green linen shirt dress cinched at the waist with a gold cord belt.

"Hi, Kathleen," said Jennifer.

The critic's dark hair was pulled back tightly, revealing a pale, aristocratic face. She pressed her lips nervously together. Intuitively, Jennifer sensed a guarded, withdrawn personality.

"May I bring you anything?" Jennifer said, responding at once to the deep sorrow she sensed in Kathleen.

"Yes," Kathleen said in her clipped, cultured voice. "Tea with lemon."

"Okay."

"And please take out the tea bag before you give it to me."

"Right."

Then Kathleen attempted a gentle smile of welcome, apparently to remove the hint of curtness in her words.

As the day progressed, Jennifer discovered the rhythm and flow of the *Times* operation. In addition to the errand running, there were piles of news releases in large manila envelopes from press agents that were dumped onto the copypersons' desk. The news releases had to be delivered promptly to a wire basket on the city desk. There were also press releases addressed individually to certain editors, such as Mike Monrony, Tom Whitney, Kathleen Owens, and others, and they had to be taken to their desks right away, too. And copypeople told her that press releases and mail

must never be allowed to stack up on the copypersons'
desk if you didn't want to get yelled at!

Of course, as she hurried through the *Times* building, Jennifer felt herself hoping that she would eventu-
ally get a chance at some news writing. But that would
come later. For the moment, it was time to keep her
eyes and ears open and learn all she could. At least she
was in the busy city room, where all the action was.

Then the blow fell.

That afternoon, she was summoned to Tom Whitney's office. "Jennifer, we're going to need a copyperson full time in the entertainment department," he told
her. "I hired you and I know you can handle the job.
So I guess you're stuck with us back here." He smiled
amiably.

Jennifer felt pleased at Tom's confidence in her, but
there was no question that she was terribly disappointed. She wanted to be part of the big news, not
movie reviews. She didn't want to work in the entertainment department, but unfortunately there was
nothing she could do about it.

As it turned out, Jennifer's job chiefly involved
waiting hand and foot on Kathleen Owens. Other
editors in the department also asked her to do projects
for them, but Kathleen's assignments seemed to take
up most of Jennifer's time.

"I don't know how things get into such a colossal
mess," Kathleen grumbled. "The place looks like a
dead-letter office." Kathleen led her to a long counter
piled with packages, large envelopes, and a massive

jumble of review record albums. "I've been doing the record review column, the 'Hot Rock Scene,' whenever the mood strikes me, but now they want it every week. That means somebody has to deal with this mountain range of records and letters."

Jennifer dived into the packages immediately, opening them and arranging the music company press releases and albums into separate piles. As she worked, she observed Kathleen closely, and the more she saw, the more curious she became. The woman was a nervous wreck, for one thing. Her hands often shook as she smoked long, thin cigarettes one after another. She never seemed to smile at all.

But late in the afternoon, Kathleen changed dramatically with the arrival of Billy Singleton. When Jennifer saw the tall, blond young man stride confidently into the entertainment department, she thought he must be a reporter, or maybe even a columnist. He went straight up to Kathleen Owens and stood there nonchalantly, as if he owned the place.

"Well, if it isn't the Dragon Lady," he said with a charming smile, and Kathleen Owens' face lit up radiantly.

"What do you want this time, Billy?" Kathleen said with a laugh. "More publicity for that broken-down band of yours, the Typewriters?"

"Just wait until they're invited to perform in Madison Square Garden," he quipped. "But don't worry, I'll send a limousine for you. Here," he said to Kathleen, inserting a long-stemmed red rose into the vase on her desk. "Happy birthday."

"It's not my birthday," she said, puzzled.

"No, it's mine. I've aged five years waiting for you to do a story on the Typewriters." He sauntered casually over to where Jennifer was putting the last of the review albums into alphabetical order on the counter. "Well, you must be Dragon Lady Junior." He grinned and Jennifer felt a blush rising to her cheeks.

"I'm Jennifer," she admitted.

"Ahhh," said Billy, smiling attractively. "The new copygirl."

"That's me."

"Pleased to meet you. I'm Billy Singleton, manager of the hottest new band in the country, the Type-writers." He moved closer, as though he were about to confide something to her. "Hey," he whispered, "how about using your influence to help a poor struggling band manager?"

Jennifer stared at him. "Me?"

"Sure, Jenny. I bet you're the real brain around here. The beauty, too."

Jennifer felt her face flush again, and a warm sensation flooded through her.

"I'm afraid you've been badly misinformed, Mr. Singleton."

"Who? Listen, Jennifer, if you're going to come out to the Cave and hear the Typewriters with me some night, it won't do to have you addressing me as though I were your uncle. Billy's the name, and music's my game." He gave Jennifer a wink and strutted out of the office.

Jennifer was dazzled, and for the rest of the day kept

smiling to herself when she thought about Billy's crazy clowning. *Was he really asking me out?* she wondered with growing excitement.

She hardly noticed Kathleen Owens rummaging through the alphabetical list of review albums and muttering that some of them seemed to be missing.

"Is this all of them, Jennifer?"

"Yes, Kathleen, all that were here."

Kathleen wagged her head in exasperation. "I tell you, you can't put anything down around here without somebody walking off with it." The music critic was staring at Jennifer, and the smile she had flashed to Billy Singleton was definitely missing.

Chapter 2

Her job on a metropolitan daily newspaper was a source of lively interest to everyone she knew, Jennifer found out almost at once. At the dinner table after her first day at the *Times,* her eight-year-old brother, Johnny, was practically bursting with questions. "What story did you cover today?" he asked.

She smiled at his interest. "No story, Johnny."

"What?" Johnny complained, brushing his sandy-colored hair out of his eyes. "But there was a big fire at the Camden Square supermarket. Didn't you go out on that?"

"Now take it easy," her mother told Johnny. "It takes time to get started. I didn't handle a case in court in my first week."

"Neither did I," added her father.

The Taggerts were law partners. Mrs. Taggert had helped put her husband through law school first, and then he had paid her way through. And all that time she was raising Jennifer and Johnny too. Jennifer always felt a surge of pride when she realized what her mother had done. It hadn't been easy, either. They had started out in a small apartment and had only succeeded in buying their own home a few years ago. The split-level ranch house was on a lovely tree-lined street on the southern edge of Springfield.

Jennifer glanced at her brother as he played with the mashed potatoes on his plate. Suddenly, he looked up and asked, "Listen, do you think you might ever cover a hockey game?"

"A *hockey* game?"

"Sure! Then if you needed anybody to carry anything for you into the press box . . ."

Jennifer laughed. "If I ever get sent out on something like that, you can be my copyboy," she said.

"That's what you are, huh?" asked Johnny. "A copyboy?"

"Copygirl," she corrected him.

"What do you do? Copy down stories for reporters?"

"You'd make a good reporter yourself, with all those questions," Jennifer said. "No. 'Copy' is a word newspapers use for stories that have been written. That's because they used to copy down stories as they were phoned in or came in over the wires. Now the word just means any written story."

Johnny gazed admiringly at his sister. "Someday I'm going to be a copyboy, too."

Johnny wasn't the only one with a lot of questions.

When Jennifer had helped clear the table and load the dishwasher, the phone rang. Johnny got to it first, as he always did, and called out that it was her friend Wendy.

"I'll take it in my room," she said and darted out of the kitchen and up the stairs to her room. It had oak-colored paneling on the walls and was decorated with framed front pages of the *Clarion* and her favorite major newspapers, *The New York Times*, *The Los Angeles Times*, and *The Washington Post*.

"Jen?" Wendy's eager voice came over the line when Jennifer had picked up her cordless phone.

"Hi, Wendy, how's it going?" Wendy Jamison was her best friend, a petite, green-eyed blonde she had known since they were both five years old.

"Don't give me that 'how's it going' stuff," Wendy bubbled into the phone. "Tell me all about it!"

"All about what?" Jennifer teased. "You mean my little silver Datsun? Let's see, the passenger door sticks sometimes, and . . ."

"Jennifer Taggert!" Wendy protested.

"You mean my job at the *Times?*"

"What else, dummy!"

"It's really great. I learned about a million things today and Kathleen Owens is something of a mystery . . ."

"Kathleen Owens, the music critic?" Wendy just about shrieked with excitement.

"That's the one."

"You *know* her?"

"Sure. I work for her."

15

Wendy sighed. "Wow! You work with the music critic who writes the 'Hot Rock Scene.' Wait till I tell everybody. I still can't believe you're on the staff of the *Springfield Times*. Especially when the rest of us have to be content with babysitting or yard work, or if we're really lucky, a job at a fantastically interesting place like Burger King."

"It was really a piece of luck, Wendy."

"Sure. The way you took over the *Clarion* was not luck! But listen, when do I get to come to the *Times?*"

"Well," Jennifer said, "maybe you could come for lunch in their cafeteria one day."

"How about tomorrow?"

"You're impossible, Wendy Jamison. But actually, my second day at work isn't a great time to have a guest. Let's make it Friday."

"I'll see you at noon."

"How about twelve forty-five, after the first dead-line? I'll tell Danny, the security guard, that you're coming to see me. Meet me by the Editorial sign on the seventh floor."

By Friday, Jennifer had the routine in the entertain-ment department down pat. Tom Whitney wanted a black coffee on his desk when he came in, and Kathleen wanted tea with lemon. *And no tea bag,* Jennifer reminded herself.

She also made it her business to bring coffee to Ellen Carroll, the movie critic, and to Joe Davis, the science writer who sat in the corner behind a stack of newspapers and scientific books of all kinds. Then she quickly sorted the mail and the press releases, distributing them so the editors and writers would have them when they came in.

That morning Kathleen walked in looking pale and reserved, but brightened when she saw the container of tea waiting for her. "I see you're learning fast," Kathleen said and smiled, sipping the hot tea and studying her young assistant. Jennifer noticed a lovely gold chain around Kathleen's neck. "That's a beautiful necklace," she said, peering closely at a small disc hanging from it. Then she noticed the name Sally engraved on it.

Kathleen involuntarily clutched at it for a moment, covering it up, but then let her hand drop. "Yes," she said. "It was my daughter's."

"Does she want to be a writer, too?" Jennifer asked pleasantly, and was surprised to notice an embarrassed flush coloring Kathleen's neck and face.

"She . . . lives in Chicago," Kathleen said, and immediately changed the subject. "Tom tells me you worked on your school paper. Do you know how to do picture captions?"

"Oh, sure," said Jennifer. "I used to make up the paper. I did layout, wrote headlines, everything."

"Good," said Kathleen. "The record column is going to start taking more of my time. I'll need you to help out by writing picture captions for some of the feature sections. Marjorie Collins, the women's editor, wants you to try writing captions for her, too. Why don't you take a look at what she has, and if you can handle it I'll give you a few music feature pictures later."

Happy to be given the opportunity, Jennifer wrote captions for three pictures that day. At the *Clarion*, she had written plenty of captions that ran underneath pictures, describing who was in the photo and what they were doing. It was a beginning, anyway, a step toward writing.

One of the captions called for a concise description of a wild linen jumpsuit, striped and double-breasted, with pants that ended somewhere between the ankle and midcalf. It was for the "Beauty and Fashion" section, which was part of the Sunday paper.

The trick to writing captions, as Jennifer had learned while sweating over them at the *Clarion*, was to make them short. There was only so much space, and you had to count the exact number of letters that would fit. For the linen jumpsuit, she had only sixteen spaces. After several tries, she finally got it. "Way-out Stripes!" she printed neatly. Marjorie Collins looked over her shoulder and grinned. "On the button," she chuckled.

The other two captions were for Kathleen's music feature, one for a photo of David Bowie and one for a photo of the Police. Both groups were appearing on upcoming cable-television rock concerts.

For one Jennifer wrote: "David Bowie: in concert on HBO."

For the other: "The Police: rocking on Showtime."

18

Kathleen quickly glanced at them and nodded approval.

So far, so good, Jennifer told herself elatedly as she hurried out to the reception area to meet Wendy for lunch. Wendy jumped up from a couch beside the reception desk and darted over to her. "Okay, super reporter, I'm starved. I hope the cafeteria has good food."

"It's excellent and not too expensive, either," Jennifer replied.

The girls took the elevator to the fourth floor, and went into the *Times* cafeteria, where they ordered chicken club sandwiches and iced tea. Glancing around from their table near the door, Wendy seemed very impressed.

"This place is great," Wendy said. "Hey, isn't that her now?" she hissed at Jennifer.

"Who?"

"Kathleen Owens."

Jennifer glanced up to find the tall, aristocratic woman walking through the cafeteria carrying a cup of tea. "That's Kathleen," she said.

"She looks just like Meryl Streep." Wendy was right. Kathleen Owens *did* look regal and rather intimidating. Wendy, her green eyes dancing, stared at her friend with admiration. "It must be terrific to work here," she sighed. "You're really on your way. So do you still have time to come out and visit an old country friend?"

Wendy lived on a small farm her parents owned in

Holly Hills, outside Springfield. She had been after Jennifer for ages to come out and ride the two new horses her father had bought. "The horses are beauties!" Wendy continued enthusiastically. "A sorrel mare and a gray gelding. Dad is so *proud*. You've got to come take a ride."

"I'd love to and I will," Jennifer promised, "but not this weekend. I'm already bushed and I want to be fresh for work on Monday." First, she resolved, she would work hard to make a good start at the paper. That was her most important priority. After that she could relax.

That afternoon she was moving quickly through the corridor, on her way from getting tea and coffee, when she almost ran down Billy Singleton as he stepped off the elevator.

"Excuse *me!*" Billy leaped back dramatically. "Look out!" he yelled in wild exaggeration, and Jennifer burst out laughing in the middle of a bright red blush. "It's the three-ten express from the cafeteria!"

"You nut," she laughed.

"Better to be a nut than get mashed into peanut butter." He smiled. "Hey, I'm going your way. I've got some candy for Kathleen." He indicated a box tied with a red ribbon. As they walked, Billy gently put his arm around Jennifer's shoulder.

"Billy, how did you get to be such good friends with Kathleen?" she asked. Despite their age difference, Billy and Kathleen almost seemed to be having a romance, with the flowers and the candy and all.

20

Jennifer liked Billy a lot, but she certainly didn't want to get involved with her boss's boyfriend.

"Well," Billy said, "I first came in here trying to get some press for the Typewriters. That's how I met Kathleen. I liked her. And she seemed so lonely and depressed. So I figured I could cheer her up a little with the presents and the jokes. She's kind of like a favorite aunt to me." He paused. "Besides, it hasn't hurt the Typewriters to have a music critic interested in them. I mean, Kathleen would never write good reviews for them if she didn't honestly like them, but I know she does more articles on them because of me."

"Here we are," Billy said, slipping his arm from Jennifer's shoulder and pushing open the door to the entertainment department. He walked right over to Kathleen's desk and plopped the box of candy down on it. "See that?" he said. "That's to remind you that you're not only as sweet as candy, but you also look like a Christmas present, too, Dragon Lady." Kathleen laughed and shook her head helplessly.

That was another nice thing about Billy. After he swept through the office like a blond Adonis, Kathleen would be in a jovial, laughing mood, instead of her usual tense, withdrawn self.

After he finished talking to Kathleen, he came over to the counter where Jennifer was working and sat down in a swivel chair. He chatted with her as she filed and marked the record albums. From time to time, he even helped her, going through the newest packages and sorting them out.

"You don't have to do that," she said shyly.

"Hey! Remember who's the music expert here," he said. "Besides, I've got to see what the competition is sending in." Then he tossed his blond head back, laughed, and started out of the office. Just as he reached the door, he looked back and said, "When are we going to the Cave, Jen? I'm sick of you turning me down." Then with a wink he was gone.

Jennifer hadn't really "turned him down," because he hadn't really asked her. Was he teasing? She didn't know. Billy was a mystery. An exciting mystery that caused her heart to skip. And what was more, he seemed to be genuinely interested in her. At first, she hadn't believed it, but she knew now it wasn't completely her imagination.

Happily, she went back to her work, making a list of all the review record albums and cross-referencing them with the artists' names. As she worked, she hummed contentedly.

Kathleen looked up quickly. "What's that?" she asked.

"What?"

"That tune you're humming. Usually we don't like humming in the newspaper, Jenny, but you seem to have a bit of an ear."

Kathleen Owens was being almost warm! "Oh, that's by the Orangemen! I really like them."

"Hmmm," said Kathleen, sipping her tea. "The Orangemen, is it? Tell you what, Jenny. I think I'll review an album by them today. Do we have one?"

"Sure! 'Big Bend Moon.' "

"Right. And, let's see . . . bring me two more . . . that new Michael Jackson album. And, uh, 'Under Water' by the Frogs."

"Okay!"

Jennifer was still humming as she walked over to the counter where she had carefully filed the albums. Kathleen seemed finally to be warming up to her a little. It was important to Jennifer to be liked and to have a pleasant working relationship with others.

Digging into the file of record albums, she flipped to O for Orangemen. But "Big Bend Moon" wasn't there. *Darn it,* she thought, *now where did I put it?* She quickly checked her master list. There it was, written in her own neat hand. She checked the cross-reference list of artists' names. It was entered there, too. She could hear Kathleen humming the refrain from the Orangemen as she continued looking. But it was no use. She couldn't find "Big Bend Moon." She had no problem locating the Michael Jackson album, which had just come in, but "Under Water" was missing, too. Thinking quickly, Jennifer brought the Michael Jackson album over to Kathleen, substituting a new Van Halen record for the Frogs' album.

"I'm still looking for the Orangemen," she said hurriedly, "but why don't you review this one instead? I hear Van Halen's getting pretty hot." Jennifer held her breath as the music critic looked up at her.

"Really?" Kathleen said, staring a little too long at Jennifer. After a pause she continued, "Actually, I think I just have room in the column to review two. So I guess I'll do the Orangemen and the Frogs next week."

With a sigh of relief, Jennifer returned to her desk, telling herself sternly that she'd go over the records carefully as soon as possible to make sure everything else was in the right place.

But the following day, when she looked in the file to begin her inspection, she gasped in surprise. There were "Big Bend Moon" and "Under Water"—filed right where they were supposed to be. For a second, Jennifer felt as though she'd been kicked in the stomach. What was going on? Yesterday those albums had definitely been missing. Today they were definitely back.

Who had returned them?

Chapter 3

After her first week at the *Times*, Jennifer realized it had been a blessing in disguise to be assigned to the entertainment department. Working for Kathleen Owens, she found herself being asked to write more and more captions and to look over stories and proofread them.

The following Monday Kathleen brought her over to one of the video display terminals. A VDT was simply a typewriter keyboard attached to a television screen, so that whatever you wrote appeared in lighted letters on the screen, just as though it were a sheet of paper in a typewriter.

But it was much easier to make changes and corrections on it, so all the reporters used them to write stories.

"Jennifer," said Kathleen, "I'm really swamped with the sections today. There's a story here about the

Springfield Symphony's concert on Sunday and it's too short. Here's some press information about the concert. Do you think you could write three more paragraphs?"

"I'll certainly try," she answered, moving over to the machine and sitting in front of it.

"Here," said Kathleen, showing her how to use it. "You just push this 'command' button, and the story will appear on the screen." Kathleen pushed the button, and there was the story. "Now, you push this 'page forward' button, and the story will move along through the screen," Kathleen explained. "You see, the keyboard is just like a typewriter, and I know you can type."

"Okay," Jennifer responded, eager to begin.

She read the story, then checked the clippings about the orchestra and the concert. She found it was simple enough to add the names of the soloists and their musical backgrounds, and to write that the concert was for the benefit of the Haley Day Care Center.

On Wednesday, Kathleen asked Jennifer for a new Culture Club album, featuring, of course, the lead singer Boy George.

Jennifer checked her files and was amazed to discover that the album wasn't there. Apparently, people were strolling in and picking things up when she wasn't in the room.

She gave Kathleen another album, which caused the critic to glance at her in mild concern. "Still having trouble with those records?" she asked.

"I'm afraid so," said Jennifer. She knew it wasn't

her fault, but she also knew the missing albums made her look incompetent.

"I have an idea," said Kathleen, eyeing her for a long moment. "We'll get a file cabinet and lock them up. I realize a lot of kids around here like these new records, but this has got to stop."

Jennifer felt a curious sensation go through her as Kathleen looked at her with narrowed eyes. Clearly, she would have to take greater care from now on. Kathleen telephoned the maintenance department and ordered a metal file cabinet and two keys. It was a relief, anyway, to know that the album problem was going to be settled.

That morning Jennifer spent several hours carefully filing the albums in the new cabinet, and checking the list of records and the cross-reference index of the names of performing artists. She finished just in time to dash out and across Manchester Avenue to the Lantern Restaurant to meet Wendy for lunch.

"Well, how's my pal, the horsewoman?" she asked cheerily as she slid into a booth opposite her blond friend.

"Lonely," Wendy replied promptly. "I told the horses a certain friend was coming out to visit, and she didn't show up."

"I'll visit you this weekend," Jennifer said. "I promise! Last weekend I was just too bushed."

"Great," said Wendy.

They ordered deluxe cheeseburgers with everything, and Jennifer found herself eating away as if she were starved.

"This job obviously calls for nourishment," Wendy giggled, rolling her green eyes. "So have you taken over the 'Hot Rock Scene' column yet?"

"Well, I'm gradually doing more writing," Jennifer told her. "But you know, I'm worried about Kathleen Owens. Wendy, she seems so sad, so depressed at times. Here she is, a successful, respected career woman. She's strikingly beautiful, but sometimes she seems like a person who's lost her last friend."

"Why do you think she's so unhappy?"

Jennifer shook her head, pondering it. "I wish I knew. About the only person who can make the Dragon Lady smile is Billy Singleton."

"Dragon Lady?"

Jennifer laughed. "That's what Billy calls her. He's always saying nutty things to her and she just laps it up."

Wendy couldn't miss noticing the way her friend's face lit up. "You really like this guy, don't you?"

"I could, but I doubt if I'll get the chance, Wendy. I told you how good-looking he is, plus he's older than I am and he manages a rock group. Why in the world would he be interested in me?"

"If you're fishing for a compliment, Jennifer Taggert, I'm not biting," Wendy said with a grin. "You've never had trouble getting dates. My money's on you."

"Thanks, Wendy. I hope you're right," Jennifer said, glancing at her watch. "Hey, look at the time! I've got to run."

"Don't forget you're coming out to the farm on

Sunday to go riding," Wendy called as Jennifer rushed out of the Lantern.

Late that afternoon, close to quitting time, Jennifer was reading the *Times,* enjoying the sight of her own picture captions in print. Sensing that someone was watching her, she glanced up. It was Billy Singleton. He always seemed to materialize out of thin air.

"It's too late for you to be getting any of these coffee fiends a cup, so I thought I'd find you here," he cracked. Dressed in jeans, cream-colored shirt, and leather tie under a military-style jacket, Billy plopped himself down on her desk top.

His nearness and the casual way he had of leaping immediately into a conversation always made an impression on her that she couldn't quite sort out.

Already his hand was on hers lightly. He sat on the desk, smiling down at her with those radiant blue eyes, his blond hair falling slightly over one eye. Being around Billy was a challenge even for someone as quick-witted as Jennifer.

"Billy," she protested with a laugh, "are you trying to tell me I'm just a glorified waitress?"

"If so, you're the prettiest one I've ever seen." He winked. "Now listen," he went on. "I'm sick and tired of being rejected. You look like a lady who belongs at the Cave listening to my group."

Think of something clever to say, Jennifer told herself. *Think of* anything *to say!* When nothing popped into her mind, she glanced around at Kathleen's desk. "Kathleen's out somewhere," she managed.

"I'm not here to see Kathleen," he said. "I'm here to see you." Jennifer looked away. She simply couldn't figure Billy out. She looked back and saw eyes filled with sincerity. "How much longer do you have to stick around here?" Billy asked. Jennifer glanced at the wall clock. It was nearly six. "Just a few more minutes. Why?"

"How would you like to grab a bite to eat and then go over to the Cave? I'll follow you home in my car, then you can drop off your car and we'll drive to the Cave, okay?"

"Sounds great to me," she said, her heart pounding with excitement at the thought of a date with Billy. Within minutes, Jennifer had locked the review record cabinet, put the key in her purse, straightened up her desk, and was ready to leave.

As she drove home, Jennifer checked her rear-view mirror every few minutes to make sure Billy was still behind her. Each time, he waved and sounded his horn lightly. And he was still there, right behind her, as she pulled into the long driveway at the side of her house.

"Very nice," he commented, his eyes taking in the house, the well-kept lawn, the carefully pruned azalea bushes, and the huge old oak tree. "Very nice, indeed."

"Thanks, Billy. Gardening is my father's hobby. He says it helps him relax after a day in court," she explained, leading him up the brick walk to the front door. "Come on in and meet my folks. It'll just take me a few minutes to change."

30

"Mom!" she called out, drawing Billy into the living room. "Dad! Why don't you sit down, Billy?" she said, motioning to a long, low sofa.

"Hi, honey, how was your day?" her mother asked as she came into the room. "Oh, I didn't know we had company."

Jennifer's resemblance to her mother was immediately obvious. Both had rich dark-brown hair, although Mrs. Taggert's was shorter. They had the same lovely brown eyes and high cheekbones, too.

"Hi, Mom. My day was just fine," Jennifer said, giving her mother a quick kiss on the cheek. "And this is Billy Singleton. We met at the office."

"How do you do, Billy." She extended her hand as Billy rose quickly from the sofa.

"Hello, Mrs. Taggert. It's very nice to meet you." They shook hands, and Jennifer noticed her usually reserved mother respond to Billy's warm, friendly smile.

"Billy and I are going out to dinner, Mom. I hope that doesn't upset your plans for dinner?"

"No problem, Jennifer. I was just putting together some leftovers and working on a brief at the same time," she chuckled. "I think the brief will be better than the dinner." Jennifer knew she could always count on Mom to be understanding.

"I'll be down in ten minutes, Billy," she said as she headed for the stairs. In her room, she quickly changed into black jeans, black low-heeled shoes, and a pink-and-white striped shirt.

Billy smiled in approval as she rejoined him in the

31

living room ten minutes later. "Very pretty," he said, taking her hand.

The bite Billy promised her turned out to be fettucine Alfredo at Guido's, the best Italian restaurant in Springfield. Sitting across the small candlelit table from Billy, Jennifer tried hard to relax. *Why am I nervous?* she chided herself. *I've been out with guys before. But none as special as Billy,* she admitted silently.

"Hey, Jen, is something wrong?" he asked, picking up on her mood. "Is the Dragon Lady doing a number on you?"

Surprised, Jennifer looked more closely at Billy. For a guy who seemed breezy much of the time, he seemed to have unusually sharp perceptions.

"I wonder about her, Billy," she admitted. "She confuses me at times."

Billy's hand found hers, and he gave her a reassuring squeeze, sending a warm tingle through her. "I don't think Ms. Owens has ever been the most outgoing type, you know?" he said. "But she has her reasons."

"Reasons? What reasons? Tell me, Billy," she insisted. Maybe if she understood Kathleen, she could help her.

"Well, Kathleen and I had a pretty serious talk at last year's Christmas party at the office. She told me she had gotten a divorce two years ago and I guess it was pretty messy."

"Oh. That's too bad."

Billy held up his hand. "Wait, there's more.

Kathleen has a daughter your age, Sally. Last year, the girl made the decision to live with her father. Kathleen's hardly seen her since then."

"That must have hurt," said Jennifer, recalling the impulsive way Kathleen had clutched Sally's necklace.

"Yeah," said Billy. "For a while, she was walking around so spaced out she hardly knew what she was doing. I think they almost let her go."

"Really?"

Billy nodded gravely. "She's better now, but still pretty nervous and jumpy sometimes."

So that's it, thought Jennifer. *Kathleen Owens is nervous because she's insecure and afraid of making a mistake.*

Jennifer and Billy sat in silence, lost in their own thoughts.

"Billy," she said tentatively, "I don't want to sound like some dumb amateur psychologist, but . . ." Her voice trailed off. She didn't want Billy to laugh at her.

"But what?" he encouraged.

"Do you suppose the fact that I'm at the office upsets her? I mean, maybe I make her think about how much she misses her daughter?"

Billy smiled and stretched his fingers across to brush an unruly lock of brown hair from her cheek. "I don't think you're an amateur at all. I think you might be absolutely right." Then suddenly the waiter appeared at their table.

"Ahhh, here's our cappuccino," Billy announced,

33

breaking the romantic spell. The familiar teasing glint was back in his blue eyes. Kathleen Owens was forgotten. "You are going to be absolutely swept away by the Typewriters, Jen," he promised. "I know now that we were fated to meet."

"What do you mean?" Jennifer said, trying hard to follow him.

"Don't you see? I subconsciously named my group the Typewriters because of you."

Jennifer surprised herself by throwing back her head and laughing out loud. Other restaurant patrons looked their way as Billy joined in. "Do you ever get serious, Billy, and how in the world did you get to be a manager?" *And when,* she asked herself, *have I ever had so much fun?*

"Do you know, that's the first time you've asked me about myself, Jen? I'm flattered." He sounded almost wistful. "But that's at least a two-record album. We'll spin it later, okay?" He was back in his role of "Billy's the name, and music's my game." Jennifer wouldn't have minded staying at the quiet restaurant all evening, but Billy quickly asked for the check and it was time to leave.

Nothing could have prepared her for the Cave. The place must have been a loft once, because it was huge, with high ceilings. A crazy cave effect had been achieved by constructing stalactites from the ceiling downward, which were met by stalagmites rising from the floor. Strobe lights darting across the ceiling gave the effect of bats zipping around between slivers of hanging rock.

"This is too much," she giggled as Billy led her along a path between what looked like bubbling pools of purple lava. That was a lighting effect, too, it turned out. Billy put his arm around Jennifer's waist and guided her toward the only empty booth along the wall of the large room, waving, shaking hands, and exchanging quips with everyone they passed. She could hardly hear him over the thumping beat the Typewriters were laying down. "How can you talk in here?" she laughed as they sat down.

"It's okay. Since you can't figure out what anybody says, everybody sounds brilliant," he said with a chuckle. Jennifer grinned back. She loved his laugh, so open and free, and the way his blond hair fell casually over his forehead.

After they had each had a Coke and listened to the band a little, Billy asked her to dance. "Listen, your purse may not be safe lying here in the booth," Billy said. "The club manager is a friend of mine. I'd better stash it in his office."

Moments later, they were on the dance floor. Billy moved like a tiger ready to pounce, his powerful dancing matching the pounding drumbeats exactly. After a few fast songs, the Typewriters went into a slow number. Gently, Billy took Jennifer in his arms and she felt as though her insides were melting. By now she was glad they had left the restaurant. Moving gracefully around the dimly lit dance floor as lights darted colored shafts around them, Jennifer felt deliciously lightheaded. With Billy's strong arms around her, his cheek against hers, she was both excited and relaxed at the same time. The music was slow and romantic.

"What's the name of this song?" she murmured.

"That's 'Pretty Face,' " said Billy. "It must have been written just for you." And then, in the half-darkness, Billy kissed her cheek. "Pretty Face," he said softly. "That's who you are, Jen, my Pretty Face."

I wish this moment could last forever, Jennifer thought happily.

Chapter 4

The glorious evening sped by so quickly that Jennifer was astounded when she checked her watch and saw that it was almost eleven o'clock. "I hate to say it, Billy," she murmured. "But I do have a midnight curfew and the *Times* will be waiting for me tomorrow."

"I understand. Wait here while I get your purse from the owner's office." He slid out of the booth and walked off toward the front of the club. Jennifer, feeling she had had about enough of the noise and lights for one night, decided to follow so he wouldn't have to come back for her. She picked her way slowly through the shadowy, smoky labyrinth, and had just reached the lobby area when she halted abruptly.

A man was standing at the door of the office, holding her purse. And it was open! Billy was just ahead of her, crossing toward the office.

"Billy!" she cried out.

He turned sharply and looked back at her, surprised to see she was so close behind him. "What's the matter?"

Jennifer darted to his side and pointed. "That man! He has my purse!"

Suddenly the man in the office door, broad-shouldered, red-faced, and powerful-looking, shot a look at them and snapped the purse shut.

"Hey, you!" Billy shouted, and broke into a run. Suddenly the man threw her purse across the floor at Billy's feet. When Billy stooped to pick it up, the big man dashed through the front door and disappeared into the darkness.

Like a cat, the band manager tore after him, but at the door he halted, peering helplessly into the night. The man had vanished. He turned, hurried back to Jennifer, and handed her her purse.

"The creep . . . he got away," Billy complained, breathing hard.

"He had it open," Jennifer blurted fearfully and immediately began checking the contents.

"Anything missing?" Billy said anxiously, hovering beside her.

Quickly she went through her belongings. Her wallet was there and no money was missing. Her house keys, her precious *Times* press card, her file cabinet key, all were there.

"Doesn't look as though he got anything," she breathed in relief. "He must have just picked it up when I saw him."

38

Billy let out a breath. "Whew! Well, that's good, anyway," he said. "I guess the bouncer was taking a break or something, and that's why no one was at the front door."

"Why did the manager leave his office open?" Jennifer asked.

"I'm sure he didn't," Billy replied. "He never does; the thief must have picked the lock."

"Did you recognize him?" Jennifer asked.

Billy looked disgusted. "No, I'm sorry to say. I know most of the people here, but not that bum. Listen, I'm sorry."

"Sorry? It wasn't your fault. You got it back for me."

Outside, Billy glared up and down the street in front of the Cave, looking for the man, but they didn't see anyone like him. There were only other club patrons leaving and arriving. After Billy spoke to the manager, they walked out to his sleek red Mustang and climbed in.

As he pulled out of the parking lot, Billy slid a cassette into his tape deck, flooding the cozy car with soft, romantic music. It was Billy Joel, singing, "I love you just the way you are . . ."

"I like some of the old quiet ones . . . at the right time," he said, and Jennifer felt his arm around her shoulder again. She snuggled closer. "Jenny?" he said softly.

"Hmmm?" she answered, not wanting to break the romantic spell with words.

"Do you really have to go home right now?"

"I should," she sighed. "I really should. It's late, and tomorrow . . ."

"Is a working day," he finished. "I know, but would another half hour make a difference?"

"I guess not. Why?"

"We really didn't get a chance to talk at the Cave."

"Talk?" she laughed. "Billy, it was almost impossible even to *think* while the Typewriters were on stage."

"You didn't like them?" He sounded disappointed.

"Oh, no! I loved them," she quickly reassured him. "They're a great group. You must be proud of them."

"Yeah, I am. But I don't want to talk about them or their gigs, or the Cave. It's a great night. How about a drive?"

"A drive? To where?"

"Silver Point."

"Well . . ." She hesitated. Silver Point was a scenic lookout on MacKenzie Hill overlooking the river. It was the most popular lovers' lane in Springfield. But Billy had been a perfect gentleman all evening and Jennifer somehow knew she could trust him. Billy only wanted to talk.

"Jenny?"

Admit it, she told herself. *You don't want the evening to end.* "I think Silver Point sounds fine," she finally said.

Billy turned the Mustang at the next corner, sweeping onto MacKenzie Drive, which led gently up over the rise toward Silver Point. He parked at the top of the rise, and they could see the lights of the city playing on the water.

"I love the view from here," Jennifer sighed.

"You come up here a lot?" She couldn't tell if he was teasing or surprised.

"We usually come here once a week in the summer. As a matter of fact, we've been doing it for years."

"Years!" The word seemed to explode from his mouth.

"Sure. There's a little park about five hundred yards that way," she said, pointing to the right.

"Park?"

"It's our family's favorite picnicking spot."

"Picnicking?" he said, as if it were a foreign word. Then he laughed. "I thought you had been here for other reasons."

"What other reasons?" she teased, looking at him, her brown eyes wide with innocence.

Billy smiled. "This reason." His kiss was gentle on her lips and she felt happiness flooding through her. Then he leaned back and smiled at her. "Your family really came up here for picnics?"

"Oh, sure," said Jennifer, "ever since I was little. Didn't your family ever bring you up here for cookouts?"

Billy laughed sarcastically. "My family definitely was not into picnics." He dropped her hand and lit a cigarette. For several moments he sat quietly against the door on his side, and she could only see his face when the cigarette glowed.

"Did I say something wrong?"

When Billy didn't speak for a moment, Jennifer was afraid she had somehow offended him. Then he turned and gave her one of his usual dazzling smiles. "No, Jennifer, you didn't say anything wrong. I have a feeling our families aren't anything alike." He stroked her cheek lightly.

"All families are different," she murmured.

"I saw your house on Webster Avenue," Billy muttered. "Well, I grew up on Collins Avenue." *That was the rough section of Springfield,* Jennifer thought to herself.

"And you said that both your parents are lawyers." She nodded. "My father split when I was four years old and my mother scrubbed office building floors for a living."

"Oh, Billy!"

"I hung out with a gang when I was in high school, and my older sister has been arrested three times for shoplifting," he said, watching her face for a reaction.

Jennifer tried to hide her shock. "Billy, you seem so different . . ."

"I *am* different, Jenny," he cut in, "and I don't live on Collins Avenue any longer. I'm going to make something of myself, something big, too," he said with conviction.

Jennifer looked at him with new eyes. *He should be bitter,* she thought. *But he isn't. He's determined.* "I think you're wonderful," she said.

"So are you, Pretty Face, so are you," he said softly with a slow, sweet smile. "You always look pretty, but

I think I like you best with the moonlight shining in your hair." His lips were just inches from hers as he spoke, and then they were covering hers in another gentle kiss.

"Oh, Billy," she sighed, loving the way his mouth felt on hers.

He shifted away from the steering wheel and pulled her into his arms. Jennifer lost all sense of time. The rest of the world ceased to exist. "You're sweet, Jenny," he said softly. Finally and reluctantly, it seemed to Jennifer, Billy released her from his arms. "I think," he said after a long moment, "that it's time for me to take you home."

Later, lying in bed and reliving each magical moment of the evening, Jennifer wondered if it was possible to fall in love that quickly.

The next morning, as Jennifer was beginning her workday, Tom Whitney walked by and saw that she was reading *The Washington Post*. "Come on in and tell me how you're doing," he called. Jennifer took her coffee carton and walked into his glass-walled office. "Kathleen tells me you're a caption-writing whiz," he said, hanging up the jacket of his gray suit. He rolled up his sleeves and sat down, propping his long legs up on his desk.

Jennifer blushed and smiled. "I've been helping out when I can. I'd really like to do a real story, though. Maybe a feature." She grinned at him. "Any hints for me?"

"Sure," he said, leaning back in his chair. "Try

something for a Sunday piece. There's always space to fill. There are stories all over. You have to get into the habit of noticing things as possible stories. When you see something unusual, something that you'd like to know more about, it's a good bet that our readers would like to, also."

"Okay," she said. "I'll keep my eyes open." She glanced out of the office and saw Kathleen arriving at her desk. "Thanks for the hints," she said and hurried out.

That weekend, Jennifer finally felt secure enough about her job to accept Wendy's invitation to go riding at the farm in Holly Hills. She felt positively liberated driving the silver Datsun along Circle Drive to the edge of Springfield. Romantic, pleasant memories of Billy floated through her mind as she listened to one of her favorite songs on the radio.

Turning off into Holly Hills, she drove the two miles to Wendy's wonderful, sprawling gingerbread-style house. It was an old wooden two-story building, with a porch that ran all the way around it on the ground-floor level. As she pulled into the driveway, Wendy came bounding off the porch to greet her.

"Jen! Jen!" she shrieked, her green eyes flashing. "You made it! I was just going to send out the blood-hounds!"

Wendy hardly allowed Jennifer to put down her purse in the front hall before she dragged her out to the corral in back. "Aren't they beautiful!" she cried, pointing to two young creatures.

Jennifer looked at the strong, proud animals, a reddish-brown mare with light-brown mane and tail, and a gray gelding. The horses looked around curiously at the two girls.

"The brown one is Duchess, and the gray one is Lancer," Wendy explained. "Come on!" She ran to a small tack room at the side of the corral. Inside, hung over a rail, were two rich brown saddles, a Western one used by Wendy's father and an English one for Wendy. Wendy had been riding for several years, first on stable horses and now on the Jamisons' own two mounts.

For Jennifer, riding was still an adventure. She had ridden maybe a dozen times, so she was hardly the horsewoman Wendy was.

"You're the guest, so you can have the good saddle," Wendy told her.

Jennifer paused. "Which one is the 'good' one?" she asked uncertainly.

"Mine . . . the English saddle," laughed Wendy.

"Oh, that's all right," Jennifer chuckled. "I'll take the Western one. There's more to hang on to."

"Okay," said Wendy, leading her back to the corral. "You get Duchess, and I'll get Lancer."

It took a few minutes to get their horses bridled and saddled, but pretty soon the girls had mounted and were ready to go. "Okay," Wendy cried, "Seventh Cavalry moving out!" Wendy and Lancer led the way out of the corral, trotting slowly along, with Jennifer and Duchess behind them.

Jennifer felt exhilarated on the powerful mare's

broad back. The day was lovely, with a few clouds floating in a perfect blue sky. The girls rode down a gently sloping grassy field, across a meadow rich with daffodils, and then down another slope to a stream that curled through the field.

When the horses had drunk their fill from the stream, they went on, up a slope to the crest of a hill. There they halted, turned the horses around, and looked back. In the distance was Wendy's house. To the east lay the haze of the city. Farther down the slope from the hill, they came to more high grass. Suddenly Jennifer felt Duchess shy to one side and pull up.

"Easy, Duchess," she said. "What's wrong?" She looked through the high grass and saw rusty railroad tracks. "Wendy," she called out, pointing. "Look!"

Wendy trotted her horse closer. "Railroad tracks," she said. "I've never seen those before."

"I wonder where they go," said Jennifer, her curiosity aroused. "Let's follow them."

They moved the horses slowly through the grass alongside the slowly curving, rusted tracks. The old railroad led them around a clump of oak trees and into a clearing. There in the distance was a pond and beside it was a crumbling old building.

"What's that?" Jennifer asked, standing in the stirrups and craning to see.

"I don't know," said Wendy, who was also trying to get a better look.

"Let's go see!" said Jennifer, and off she and Duchess went, cantering through the clearing. Wendy and Lancer raced after them.

As they drew nearer, the grassy slope gave way to gravel, broken paving, and stretches of cobblestone. The rusty tracks ran through the clearing to the old ramshackle building that stood on the edge of a pond. Jennifer reined in her mare and walked the animal slowly up to the building. Wendy rode cautiously beside her. They looked up at the crumbling old brick building. It was seven stories high, with a decaying wooden office in front, perched on a splintered wooden loading platform. The railroad spur ran along the loading platform. Across the top of the great brick structure was a long sign, its painted letters chipped and peeling. STANLEY ICE COMPANY, it read.

"I know where we are," Wendy suddenly exclaimed. "It's the old Stanley icehouse! We're at Miller Pond."

"An icehouse!" said Jennifer, enthralled at the sight of the crumbling old building. It seemed to her like an abandoned fort that belonged in an adventure story.

"My dad told me it was out here someplace," said Wendy. "He said they used to make ice here years ago. They used to ship ice out of here for the Union Army in the Civil War."

Jennifer urged Duchess closer to the sagging wooden office on the loading platform that ran along the building. A large sign was posted there: DANGER! CONDEMNED!

A vanished world sprang up in Jennifer's active

47

mind as she gazed on the relic of another time. She imagined ice trucks, and even ice wagons pulled by teams of horses, moving in and out of the Stanley icehouse. Here was a piece of Springfield's history, crumbling, deserted, soon to be demolished. And all of it was forgotten in the little valley beyond Holly Hills. "Something unusual," she said. "Something people would like to know more about."

"What?" said Wendy, puzzled.

"Wendy . . . this is it. It's what I've been looking for—just the thing to write about. Why, it's perfect! I'd love to see the inside."

"See that big 'Condemned' sign?" Wendy cautioned.

"Yes, I see it," sighed Jennifer. "But still . . ."

After looking the place over for half an hour and becoming more and more fascinated and curious about it, Jennifer reluctantly gave in to Wendy's urgings that it was time to start for home. Riding away, she turned at the clump of trees for another look. She would be back, she told herself.

Chapter 5

Jennifer could hardly wait to get to work on Monday morning to start on her feature story about the Stanley icehouse. After the morning coffee run, she checked the Springfield telephone book. There was no listing for a Stanley icehouse, but she found one for Stanley & Company on Orchard Avenue. Jotting down the number, she walked back to her desk and dialed it.

"Stanley and Company," answered a surprisingly youthful voice.

"Hello?"

"Yes?"

"This is Jennifer Taggert . . . of the *Springfield Times*," she said. "Is Mr. Stanley there?"

"This is Mr. Stanley," the voice said, although the person sounded too young to own a company. "May I help you?"

"I'm calling about the Stanley icehouse," she said. There was a silence. Then, "What?"

"Well, sir," said Jennifer, "you see . . ."

"I've been instructed to say that there will be no comment on the case," the voice said, suddenly curt and businesslike. Then the line went dead. The person had hung up. Jennifer put the phone down. She knew being a reporter wasn't an easy job, and she'd heard that reporters often ran into problems getting a story, so she was not about to quit just because someone refused to talk to her.

On her lunch hour she hurried out of the *Times* and across the employee parking lot to the Datsun. She drove to Orchard Avenue, and after two blocks she spotted the address, 2512 Orchard Avenue, on the front of a modernistic marble and glass building.

She parked the car and entered, a little nervously. She took the elevator up to the third floor and pushed open a glass door at the end of the hall. A receptionist sitting at a white kidney-shaped desk in the carpeted office looked up at her inquiringly.

"May I see Mr. Stanley?" Jennifer asked.

"Who shall I say is calling?" the woman asked politely.

"Jennifer Taggert of the *Springfield Times*." She wasn't sure, but she thought the receptionist gave her a funny look. In a moment she was shown into an inner office.

"Is Mr. Stanley in?" she asked the brown-eyed young man seated behind a desk. He was wearing a tan

50

cotton suit and a blue shirt open at the neck. He appeared to be not much older than she.

"I'm Mr. Stanley," he said, sounding annoyed. She recognized the voice immediately. He was the one who had hung up on her! The young man had dark curly hair that appeared to need cutting, and there was something in the way he looked at her that made her uneasy. For some reason, he seemed suspicious of her. "What can I do for you?" he finally asked in a rather gruff voice.

"I'm a reporter for the *Times,*" she began, and immediately noticed the young Mr. Stanley's eyes narrow.

He sees right through me, she thought uncomfortably. *He knows I'm not really a reporter.* Then, realizing he couldn't be much older than she was, she decided to tell him the truth.

"Look, Mr. Stanley, I'm not really a reporter yet. I'm just working there for the summer."

The curt manner seemed to lessen somewhat. Mr. Stanley allowed himself a sort of smile. "Well," he said, "I'm only working in this office for the summer, too." They looked at each other and laughed. "Ken Stanley," he introduced himself. "It's my father's office."

"I wondered how . . ." Jennifer laughed. "I mean you don't look like a 'Mr. Stanley.' You do look like a Ken, though."

"I just finished Washington High three weeks ago," said Ken.

"That explains it." Jennifer smiled. "I'll be a senior at Jefferson in September. We south-siders hardly ever meet you north-siders—except when we beat you at football."

"*You* beat *us* . . . *!*" And then Ken Stanley laughed. "Well, what can I do for you? I've already told you I can't comment on the case."

"Case?" said Jennifer, totally lost.

"Isn't that why you're here?" he said, and that suspicious look was back. Then he looked away and moved a stack of papers from one side of the desk to the other. *Why is he so nervous?* Jennifer wondered.

"I don't know anything about any case," she said. "I want to talk to you about the old icehouse."

Ken Stanley once more shifted into an all-business personality. He seemed suddenly very reserved, even grudging. "It's condemned and about to be torn down," he said. "It went up in the 1880s, and was an icehouse until the 1950s. Then it became a warehouse. That's about all. It's totally deserted now."

"But didn't they supply ice to the Union Army in the Civil War?" Jennifer asked eagerly.

"No, no, that was before this icehouse. They used to cut ice from Miller Pond and store it in an icehouse. This one was built later."

"It sounds fascinating," Jennifer protested, surprised that Ken could brush off the history of the wonderful historic site in a few hurried words. "I'm thinking of doing a story about it for the *Times*," she went on, trying again.

Ken Stanley shot her a strange, frightened glance.

He looked away. "I'd have to check with my father. He's in California. I'm not sure when he'll be back."

Jennifer wondered what there was about this boy that intrigued her. He was quite interesting-looking, for one thing, with thick dark eyelashes and unruly black hair. And those brown eyes! They were a flash of friendliness one second, a curt barrier the next.

"Oh," said Jennifer. She stood up. Ken Stanley's words and manner seemed to indicate the interview was over. She moved toward the door. Quickly, Ken was on his feet and standing beside her. He was tall and athletic, and he seemed very disturbed. "I'm sorry I was so abrupt," he said, apparently embarrassed. "I'm . . . uh . . . just going out to lunch. Have you eaten?" Jennifer saw Ken Stanley's face flush with uncertainty as he rushed the words out clumsily.

"No," she said. "I haven't."

"There's a nice little place around the corner. Why don't we go together?" he said and held the office door open for her.

When they reached the street, Ken gave Jennifer a little smile. She noticed that he walked with the fluid, graceful motion of an athlete. As they crossed Eighteenth Street, he held her arm. To Jennifer, he was a mass of contradictions.

"Here we are," he said, indicating a place on the corner.

It was a charming little restaurant, the Blue Front Café, done in various shades of blue. By the time they were settled in a booth, it seemed to Jennifer that Ken Stanley had regained his lighter, friendlier mood.

53

As they munched on roast beef sandwiches and sipped Cokes, Jennifer decided she really liked Ken. She didn't usually make up her mind about someone this quickly, but he was different. Part of the reason she liked him was his shyness, which made him seem kind but unsure of himself. A few times when she looked up, she noticed him watching her, then he'd turn away and blush. *Why, his gruffness is all a big bluff to cover up his shyness,* she decided.

"Ken," Jennifer finally said, reassured by his warm, open manner, "I'd really like to do a story about the icehouse. It's a piece of history! And soon it will disappear."

It was amazing, she realized later. It was as though Dr. Jekyll turned into Mr. Hyde right before her eyes. Ken's friendliness dissolved into a glowering, withdrawn, stubborn mood. "Who sent you to snoop around?" he snapped.

"What?"

"I know about reporters. They'll do anything to get a story."

"I'm not really a reporter, yet." She was astounded at his heated reaction.

"Is that why they sent you? They thought I might talk to somebody young and attractive?"

Jennifer felt her mind racing. What a backhanded way to pay a compliment! "Nobody sent me, Ken. I just happened to be horseback riding past the icehouse one day."

Ken sat forward, his eyes burning into her. "What? You were out there?"

Amazed at his reaction, Jennifer nevertheless did not falter this time. "Yes," she said. "Before it's torn down, I'd really love to go inside and explore it."

He glared at her, his eyes hard and flat. Very deliberately, he put down his Coke. "You stay away from that icehouse," he suddenly commanded. "You hear me?" Then Ken shook his head, as though trying to rid himself of his strange mood and the words he had uttered. "I'm sorry," he said softly. "Maybe I'm wrong about you."

She leaned forward, intrigued and mystified. "Ken, I don't know what I said that upset you. I wasn't trying to, really."

"Okay," he said gently. "Okay, let's let it go, then. Just don't go hanging around there. Anything could happen. Besides," he said, relaxing a little, "I know that ugly old warehouse inside and out. If all you want is to write about the good old days, I can tell you anything you want to know." He smiled charmingly.

Jennifer felt as if her head were in a whirl. Ken Stanley was very hard to keep up with. How could he be so blunt and unfriendly and then so gentlemanly within seconds? "Ken . . ." She hesitated.

He leaned across the booth, looking with concern into her eyes. "Forgive me?" he said. "Why don't we talk the whole thing over some evening? Say . . . a week from Thursday?"

She had to smile at that. "Well . . . okay, Ken."

They walked back to Ken's office in a relaxed, happy mood. He squeezed her hand before she walked across Orchard Avenue to her car. But driving back to the *Times,* Jennifer was buffeted by waves of conflicting emotions. *He likes me,* she decided. *And I think I like him too.* But another side of her asked, *Do you understand him?* Jennifer decided to avoid that question.

The following Sunday, Jennifer returned to Holly Hills and again rode out across the wide, sweet-smelling grassy meadow with Wendy. It was another nearly perfect summer day, and Duchess and Lancer were eager to run. First Duchess pranced forward energetically and then Lancer broke into a gallop. Pretty soon, they could see the Stanley icehouse. There appeared to be some figures moving around it.

"Come on, Wendy," Jennifer called out. "Let's ride closer. I want to see the old icehouse again." She thought to herself, *Maybe I'll be able to do a feature story without going inside.*

Soon the girls came to the edge of the clearing. The dilapidated old building was dead ahead, but suddenly Jennifer saw something that made her gasp in surprise. Parked by the loading platform was a van. And there were men on the platform, going into the building. Then a large door shut behind them.

Jennifer's eyes widened. Why had Ken Stanley told her the icehouse was deserted?

Chapter 6

When the next week started at the *Times,* Jennifer was finishing the cross-indexing of some review albums that had arrived on Friday. Included were albums by Air Supply and Men at Work, which she promised herself she'd listen to as soon as Kathleen finished her review. But later that day, when Kathleen asked her for the two albums, Jennifer searched her files for them in vain. Both were missing!

"I don't understand," Jennifer said in astonishment.

"What's the matter, Jenny?" Kathleen asked, walking over to her. "Did I throw you by asking for them on a Monday instead of a Wednesday? I'm trying to build up a backlog of reviews so I won't have to work so frantically to get everything done for the Thursday column."

"No, no, that's not it. Kathleen, I don't know what to say. They're not here!"

" What aren't?"

"Those two new albums by Air Supply and Men at Work. I looked everywhere."

Kathleen lit a cigarette with shaking hands, giving Jennifer a strange look. "Didn't you lock them inside the cabinet?" she asked.

"Yes, on Friday afternoon!"

Kathleen looked very pale, as though fearing this could be blamed on her. "Jennifer," she finally said, "you aren't taking records home to listen to, are you?"

"No, Kathleen, I wouldn't do that."

"But you say you locked them inside the cabinet, and only you and I have keys."

"Maybe I misfiled them," Jennifer said unhappily. "I'll stay after work and go over every one to make sure."

"You know that you're responsible for them," Kathleen said anxiously.

Jennifer sighed unhappily. "I know," she said.

Jennifer stayed an hour after work that evening, going over every single review album and checking every cross-reference. She was determined to figure out what was happening. The missing albums made her look incompetent and irresponsible. But it was no use. A painstaking check of every album, one by one, revealed that the two review records by Air Supply and Men at Work were gone. Someone in the office *had* to be taking them. But who? And how could she, a summer copygirl, accuse one of the paper's full-time staff members? Even if she did know which person was taking the records, would anybody believe her?

But her confusion over how the albums had disappeared turned to amazement the next morning when she opened the cabinet. Automatically, her eyes fell upon the two spaces where the missing records had been. They were no longer missing. They were back!

Jennifer blinked in astonishment. For a sickening moment she wondered if Kathleen was trying to sabotage her job by making her look like a fool. Did the music critic want her fired for some reason?

Jennifer sank slowly down into the chair at her desk. At first, she had put it down to misfiling—but not anymore. And yet why would Kathleen, or anyone for that matter, go through so much trouble to take review albums from the cabinet, keep them overnight, and then return them? She tried to make sense of it, but no answers came.

A glance at her watch brought her out of her musings. Kathleen and Tom would be in soon. Jennifer made the morning coffee run and placed Kathleen's tea on her desk right next to the once-missing Air Supply and Men at Work albums.

Kathleen hurried to her desk, picked up her tea, and immediately spotted the albums. "Oh, I see you found them," she said, glancing at Jennifer sternly.

"Yes, I found them this morning."

"Were they at home?" Kathleen asked, rather severely.

"No! I told you I would never do that."

"Okay, Jenny," Kathleen sighed. "I hope there's no more of this confusion. I can't take the blame for things that go wrong around here." Jennifer noticed that Kathleen's hands were shaking.

"Oh, no, Kathleen," Jennifer assured her. "It's my responsibility. I'll figure out what's happening."

"I don't want to have to bring this up with Tom Whitney, you know," said Kathleen, stubbing out her cigarette and immediately lighting another one.

"It won't happen again, Kathleen."

The music critic nodded and looked away. "I hope not," she murmured.

Jennifer went to her desk and sipped from her coffee container, her thoughts racing. Maybe somebody else had a key. Her job was at stake—she *had* to find out who that somebody was. The maintenance department might give her a lead. Jennifer rode the elevator to the basement and walked along a hallway until she saw the building maintenance office. She hesitated at the door, then knocked and walked in.

One of the maintenance men who had brought in the metal filing cabinet was sitting at a table sipping coffee. He looked up and smiled. "Well, hello, young lady," the man said pleasantly. "What brings you all the way down here?"

"Hi!" Jennifer smiled. "I feel kind of foolish, but I think I've lost my key to the cabinet you brought into the entertainment department last week."

"Ah, that's too bad." He frowned.

"Would you by any chance have another one?"

The man made an unhappy face and shook his head.

"Oh, no. There are only two. They were very strict about that. I'll have to see Miss Owens, and . . ."

Jennifer felt her breath rush out. She put her purse quickly on the table where the man was sitting, and dug into it. Then she smiled brightly at him and laughed. "Well, would you look at that?" She brought out her key and held it up. "I had it all the time."

"Ah, well, now, that's one on you," he laughed.

"But there are no others?" she asked.

"No, I'm sure of that."

"Thanks," Jennifer said. "It's nice to know everything's secure." She smiled ironically and left.

Riding back upstairs, she felt the confusion and helplessness rise up in her again. And then another feeling took over. Anger! She was not helpless. Hadn't her mother and father taught her to approach a problem logically? She would find out what was going on if it was the last thing she ever did. Almost immediately, though, Jennifer was swept up in the day's actions and there was no time to think about it at all.

At one point, she dashed into Tom Whitney's office with a stack of photos he needed immediately. "Well," he said, "how's it going, Jenny? Any luck finding a feature story?"

Jennifer hesitated. She had put Ken Stanley and the icehouse out of her mind for that moment. She didn't want to think of him lying to her like that. "Well, Tom," she hedged, "I'm still sort of working on a possibility."

"Let me know if I can help in any way."

The conversation came to an abrupt halt when the

command "Copy!" floated across the room to Jennifer's ears. Ellen Carroll, the movie critic, wanted to borrow her for a few hours. Off Jennifer flew, catching a fleeting glimpse of Billy Singleton as she crossed the room.

"I know where you can get a pair of roller skates, Jenny," he called as she went by.

Wonderful, funny Billy. Would he ever ask her out again? she wondered. Actually, she hadn't planned on a busy social life during the summer months. She had resolved to put all her energies into her job. But suddenly there were two attractive guys interested in her. The fact that they were totally opposite types made it all the more intriguing.

So that night, when her little brother told her a boy on the phone wanted to speak to her, Jennifer wasn't sure which boy to hope was calling—blond, easygoing Billy Singleton or dark, intense Ken Stanley. It turned out to be Ken, confirming their date for Thursday night. Jennifer was amazed when he told her he'd made reservations for dinner at the Royal Oaks, Springfield's most exclusive country club. She had figured he'd take her for a burger and a movie.

On Thursday she was so nervous about her date with Ken that she could barely concentrate on her work. She'd packed her best clothes and brought them to work, since she wouldn't have a chance to go home and change before the date. Her parents had driven her to the paper that morning. She hadn't used her Datsun since Ken would have a car, and two cars on a date was one too many.

It wasn't until early in the afternoon, when Billy showed up, that Jennifer's mind left Ken. Billy strolled casually into the entertainment department, and immediately the room warmed with his charm.

"Jenny, you're a hard lady to keep up with," he said, flashing her a winning smile.

"Hi, Billy. Can you believe how hectic this place is?"

"They do unlock the doors and let you out at six, don't they?" he teased. "How would you like to make a return visit to the Cave with me tonight? I know a terrific little Greek restaurant on the way that serves a fantastic moussaka."

"I've never tried moussaka, but I'd sure like to. But . . . I'm sorry, I can't tonight, Billy. I'm busy." Darn, why couldn't he have asked her for tomorrow?

"Aha! I shouldn't be surprised to find out that such a fair maiden has other knights seeking her favors," he said, putting his hand over his heart with mock sadness, and Jennifer burst out laughing.

"Billy, you are outrageous!"

"Too outrageous to go out with another time?"

"I'd love to." Jennifer silently thanked her fairy godmother for watching over her.

"Good, then I'll pick you up here tomorrow."

"I can't wait," she said, "but just now I've got to dash. I was just bringing these proofs up to production when you came in."

"Don't let me hold the busy lady up." Billy grinned. "Mind if I use the phone?"

"You're asking me?" she laughed. "I thought you

owned this place." As Jennifer went out of the office, she could see Billy lounging in her chair, dialing a number. *Two dates with two great guys,* she thought. *This is going to be one crazy week.*

At six o'clock, Jennifer slipped into the women's rest room and put on her fancy clothes. She'd brought her favorite silk dress, a flowing, midcalf length in white and rose, and her high-heeled rose-colored sandals. Carefully, she brushed her deep brown hair and put on some eyeliner, mascara, and lip gloss. "Pretty good," she told her reflection in the mirror. She was feeling very glamorous.

But when she got to the street, she felt a little out of place. There she was in a silk dress while people rushed around her, hurrying home. Fortunately, she didn't have to wait long. Ken was right on time.

As he was helping her into his car, she noticed something out of the corner of her eye—a somehow familiar shape, moving away quickly. She looked closer. A broad-shouldered man was hurrying across the street near the corner. And then it suddenly registered.

"It's him!" she gasped.

"What?" said Ken, looking at her.

"That man crossing the street . . . he tried to steal my purse the other day."

Ken shot a look in the direction Jennifer was pointing excitedly. Even as Ken looked, the middle-aged man disappeared around the corner. "Really? He tried to mug you?"

"No, it was in a . . . place," she stuttered, wondering why she didn't want to mention Billy Singleton to Ken.

"Funny," Ken was saying, looking across the street. "I thought I recognized him for a second. But it couldn't be."

"Who?"

Ken shook his head. "He looked a little like Leonard Randolph, a guy who used to work for my father. Probably wasn't, though. He left town a year ago, right after he was fired."

"Fired?"

"Yeah. My father suspected him of stealing money from the company." Ken climbed into the car, started it, and drove away. "Did the thief steal anything?" The concern in his voice surprised and touched her.

"No," she replied shortly. Then, to change the subject, she said, "Your car is a real beauty. Wow, a white Thunderbird. It must have cost a fortune."

"No," he laughed. "This little ten-year-old gem was a disaster area when I bought it for almost nothing. It's taken me a year and a lot of hard work to get into shape. I like tinkering with cars," he admitted with a grin.

Neither of them mentioned the thief again as they drove toward the country club. They talked about movies and their rival schools, and the disturbing mood melted away. Soon they were at the club.

Jennifer had been to Royal Oaks only once before, for a friend's sixteenth-birthday party. The main dining room was as elegant as she remembered. The Waterford chandeliers sparkled; heavy white tablecloths with deep red overlays made a perfect background for gleaming white china and heavy, ornate silverware. The plush carpeting absorbed the sound of their footsteps as the maitre d' showed them to a window table overlooking the formal gardens.

But even though she enjoyed the unaccustomed richness of the surroundings and food, Jennifer felt uneasy. Jeans and pizza would have been more relaxing, she thought. The easy informality and fun of Billy and the Cave came back to her as she studied Ken's face. Was this the sort of thing he did all the time? she wondered. He certainly seemed to feel at home. He knew exactly what main course to order, and he even teased Jennifer into agreeing on escargots as an appetizer. "I don't care what you want to call them, Ken, they're still snails." Jennifer laughed.

"Afraid to try them?" he dared with a grin.

"Not on your life!"

But considerate, amusing Ken fell into sudden silences that puzzled Jennifer. *It can't be just shyness,* she reasoned. *He almost seems to be hiding something. But what?*

"I hope you have insurance on your feet," he said when he led her out onto the dance floor. The music was far slower and softer than at the Cave, but that didn't surprise Jennifer. She had already noticed that she and Ken were the youngest people there. Everyone else seemed to be about her parents' age or older.

"You're doing just fine," she said truthfully.

"Thanks. I haven't been dancing in a long time," he explained.

After a few wonderfully long, slow dances, Ken led Jennifer out to the wishing well in the garden. There was a full moon with a soft summer breeze. They sat in silence, enjoying the cool night. Then Ken put his arms around her and kissed her. His mouth was sweet and tender. *What a perfect evening*, Jennifer thought.

But the perfection was shattered on the drive home. Jennifer didn't want to spoil the romantic mood, but she needed answers about what she had seen at the icehouse. She really liked Ken, but the thought that he had lied to her still bothered her. She took a deep breath and said, "Ken, I went out to the icehouse again last Sunday."

Ken slapped his hand angrily against the steering wheel. "Didn't I tell you to stay away from there!"

Shocked by his sudden anger, Jennifer almost let the matter drop. But she was a reporter, or hoped to be one, and reporters kept probing for answers. "You told me the place was deserted."

"It *is* deserted."

"I saw men going in."

"You couldn't have," he insisted.

"I tell you, I did! Why didn't you tell me the truth?"

Ken ground his words out through gritted teeth. "I did tell you the truth! The place is condemned and my father is going to set a demolition date as soon as he gets back from California. The men you saw were probably part of the demolition crew."

"All right," she said softly, trying to calm him down. But it didn't work.

"I should have known better," he hissed angrily. "I

67

know what you're after! Well, don't expect me to help you!" When he parked the Thunderbird at her house, Ken took her up to the door, mumbled a quick "Goodnight," and walked quickly back to his car. Jennifer had never felt so bewildered.

"Guys," Jennifer muttered as she got ready for bed. "Who can figure them out? Who needs them?" She brushed her dark hair with more vigor than usual, then peered into the mirror and answered her own question. "I do. They're rotten, confusing, and impossible, but necessary," she admitted with a sigh. She jumped at the sound of the phone and grabbed it before it could wake her parents.

"Hello?"

"Jennifer, it's Ken Stanley." There was a pause. "I feel really rotten."

"I have to admit I'm a little surprised to hear from you."

"Jenny, I'm so sorry for snapping at you on the way home. I behaved like a total jerk. Will you forgive me? Will you give me another chance?"

"Ken, I don't . . ."

"Please, Jenny! Can I see you Saturday night?"

"Well . . ."

"Nothing fancy," he said. "I can only afford the Oaks once in a decade. How about pizza at Due's? Its deep-dish is the best, especially with a ton of onions."

Jennifer knew there would be no point in turning him down. She definitely wanted to see him again. Despite his strange moods, she really liked him. "I'll take onions over snails anytime, Ken."

"Thanks, Jenny, thanks for giving me another chance," he said softly.

Jennifer's dreams that night were alternately filled with a black-haired young man whose eyes seemed awfully sad at times, and a bright, sunny fellow with dancing blue eyes who called her Pretty Face. It was turning into a strange summer.

Chapter 7

Driving to the *Times* on Friday morning, Jennifer realized she had overlooked something that was right under her nose. All summer she had been dashing to the newspaper library for clippings for editors and reporters. Maybe the same library would hold some answers for her about the old Stanley icehouse. There should be stories about the place going back many years.

At lunch time, she talked to Mike Fallon, the short, chubby assistant librarian, about getting some information. "Well," he said thoughtfully, "most of the clips on an old story like that will be on microfilm. I can make some copies, but it might take a while. I probably won't get to it today."

"No hurry," Jennifer agreed.

"Okay, Jenny, see me Monday afternoon."

*   *   *

Later that day, Billy Singleton strolled into the office carrying two long-stemmed red roses. He marched over to Kathleen's desk and handed her one of them. "For you, oh great queen of critics," he said to Kathleen. "This is for the beautiful things you wrote about the Typewriters."

"Oh, Billy!" Kathleen laughed. "You sure know how to make a woman feel good."

"Why, thank you," he said, bowing low. Then he walked over to Jennifer and held out the other rose to her. "For you, fair damsel."

Astonished, Jennifer took the rose and held it up to her nose. She was blushing furiously, she realized. "It's beautiful."

"Silence," Billy went on. He took out a sheet of yellow paper and pretended to read from it. "Attention Jennifer Taggert. You are hereby ordered to attend spelunker training after work tonight." He looked up.

Totally lost, Jennifer frowned at him. "Huh?"

"You know what a spelunker is?"

"No."

"A spelunker is a person who investigates caves!"

"Caves?" she said, beginning to catch on.

"Caves," declared Billy. "One cave in particular. *The* Cave. I'll pick you up after work for moussaka, and we'll go on to the Cave later. Okay?"

"Super."

Almost before she realized what was happening, Billy leaned over and kissed her lightly on the cheek.

Then he was on his way, walking jauntily out of the entertainment department.

Billy's arrival and departure acted like a tonic for Jennifer, and the rest of the day seemed to speed by. She helped Kathleen with the layout and captions for Sunday's "Beauty and You" page, and then carefully went over the page proofs, checking every line for mistakes. She could hardly believe it was already six when she glanced up and saw Billy standing there again.

"Spelunker patrol about ready to move out," he declared.

"So soon?" Jennifer asked.

"Now or never," Billy went on.

"Okay, Caveman," said Jennifer. She straightened her desk and locked the cabinet, wondering wryly what good that did. Maybe she should hide in a corner of the entertainment department overnight and watch the cabinet. She was pondering that rather extreme measure when Mike Fallon walked in.

"Hey, Jenny," he said. "I found some clippings for you." He handed Jennifer an envelope from the library. "Get the rest from me on Monday."

"Thanks a lot for bringing them down, Mike." She quickly stashed them in her desk drawer. There was no time to read them now, with Billy standing there waiting.

It was one of those evenings when everything went just right. She discovered she loved moussaka, and she never stopped laughing, except when Billy drew

73

her out onto the floor of the Cave for dancing. He got the band to play a song just for her, and then laughed it off as nothing important.

"Jenny," he murmured against her cheek during a slow dance, "you are the kind of spelunker I'd like to get lost with in a cave."

"But, Billy, what if we couldn't find our way out?" she asked. At that moment she knew being lost in a cave with Billy would be heaven.

"Who cares?" Billy breathed. And he kissed her in the half-darkness.

Jennifer wondered if it was because Billy Singleton had been so charming and so much fun that she felt a little strange with Ken when he picked her up on Saturday night. Was she being more than usually critical? she wondered. Was she comparing the two? Was she even starting to choose? But Ken seemed different on this second date, different in a good way. He was certainly more relaxed. Maybe it was because she wasn't in a silk dress and he wasn't wearing a sports jacket. You couldn't really get to know a guy very well at a formal place like the Royal Oaks.

The pizza parlor, Due's, turned out to be a warm and friendly Italian place near the old Springfield Water Tower, a city landmark. They slid into a booth, and Ken insisted on ordering. "I know exactly what you'll like."

"Gee, do they have escargot pizzas here?" she teased.

"You're not going to let me forget that, are you?"

He grinned. He really did have a wonderful smile. The waiter came by and Ken ordered a sausage-and-onion pizza and two house salads. He smiled at her across the red-and-white checkered tablecloth. He seemed to have put on a whole new personality, not at all like the moody, gloomy boy she'd gotten to know. "Well, how's the job going?" he asked.

"Oh, it's hectic," she said, "but I love it. I'm going to hate to see the summer end."

"Yeah, me too," he said. "I can't believe it. I'll be leaving Springfield in the fall."

"To go to college?"

Ken nodded. "I've been accepted at the University of Wisconsin."

"Have you decided on a major yet?"

"Philosophy," he said. "I think I'd like to teach."

Jennifer looked gravely at him. "Yes, you do look rather professorial, Mr. Stanley." She giggled.

To her surprise, Ken laughed. "I guess I am sort of a stuffed shirt at times. It's not always easy for me to relax." He reached across and took her hands, his dark eyes shining in the dim light. "But I think you're getting me out of that."

Jennifer felt a ripple of warmth go through her. Ken was such a sweet guy. She squeezed his hand. How could she possibly choose between him and Billy?

The sausage-and-onion pizza, with a delectable crispy crust, was delivered with a flourish by the waiter. Jennifer dug in, loving the spicy taste. It was as tasty as Ken had promised.

"Hmmm?" Ken asked, his eyes questioning.

"Hmmm!" she answered affirmatively. They both laughed at their wordless communication.

All too soon, the marvelous feast was gone. Jennifer was wondering what else Ken had planned when he leaned over and spoke confidentially to her. "Jenny, how would you like to visit Alaska?"

"What?"

"And Canada?"

"Why not Moscow?"

Ken laughed. "Maybe even Moscow!"

"Sure, Mr. World Traveler." She smiled, watching his mischievous, glowing brown eyes. "But I have to be home by twelve-thirty. That's my weekend curfew."

"Not to worry," he chuckled.

Seated in the Thunderbird again, Jennifer realized what Ken's trip to Alaska and Canada would have to be. Travel pictures! She groaned inwardly. What was more agonizingly boring than pictures of strangers standing in front of cathedrals and mountains?

Ken drove down a shady residential street and soon pulled into a long driveway. "Your house?" she asked, looking out at a large, impressive Tudor-style home.

"Right," he said. But he didn't stop by the house. He drove to the rear of a darkened yard and parked the car.

Oh-oh, Jennifer thought, wondering if those dark eyes of Ken's hid a predatory nature. They were parked in almost pitch blackness under a huge old oak tree. She was waiting for him to move across the front

76

seat toward her and trying to decide what her reaction would be. That kiss by the wishing well at the Royal Oaks was one thing. But a dark car behind his parents' house was another.

But Ken opened the car door on his side, got out, and moved around to the passenger side to hold the door for her. "Come on," he said.

"Where?" she asked uncertainly. There was nothing in the dark back yard but a large garage.

"I told you. Alaska!" He was smiling again, and his face showed an innocent sincerity that persuaded her to go along with him. She slid out of the car. Ken took her hand and led her through the darkness toward the garage.

"Ken . . . ?" she said hesitantly, drawing back.

He only laughed. "It's all right, I promise you."

"Well . . ."

He moved to the garage and opened the door. Jennifer was almost going to dash back to the car when Ken snapped on a light switch just inside the door. Encouraged, she moved through the door after him. Ken walked to a corner of the garage and switched on another light over a little table. Arrayed on the table was a maze of electronic gadgets, dials, and radio components. As Jennifer examined the curious layout, Ken was already sitting on a chair at the table turning on switches. Then she saw a microphone on the table. "What in the world . . ." Ken was busily turning a dial. Static and radio sounds suddenly blipped into the garage. Thoroughly fascinated, Jennifer moved beside him and watched his swift, sure fingers at the controls of the lighted panels. "What are you doing?" she asked, amazed.

"What do you think? Arranging your trip to Alaska." Ken flipped a switch on the microphone and spoke into it.

"This is W4KSM. Do you read me, anybody?"

And then Jennifer finally understood. "Ken . . . you're a ham radio operator?"

Radio bloops and crackles popped from the equipment. "Did you think I was really going to fly you to Alaska?" He laughed, looking pleased at her surprise.

"This is W 4 King Stanley Mike calling WB2LJR. Do you read?" said Ken into the mike.

"Hi, Joe, how are you?" said a cheery voice.

Ken laughed and looked up at Jennifer. "That's the way everybody answers." He spoke into the mike again. "King Stanley Mike here. Is that you, Colin?"

"It's me, Ken! How are things in Springfield?"

"Better and better, Colin." He smiled at Jennifer. "How's Alaska?"

"Okey-dokey, Ken. I bet it's warmer there than here!"

"Colin, listen, I want you to meet a friend of mine, Jenny."

"Put her on," the cheery voice bubbled.

Ken stood up and motioned for Jennifer to sit. "Go on. Talk to Alaska."

Jennifer's mouth popped open. "That's . . . *Alaska?*"

Ken laughed. "Go on."

78

DANGEROUS BEAT

Jennifer slid into the chair and tentatively spoke into the mike. "Hello . . . Alaska? This is Jennifer Taggert in Springfield."

"Hi, Jenny! Tell Ken I reached Rio the other night."

Jennifer gasped. "Rio de Janeiro?"

Colin's laugh floated over the radio. "That's the only Rio I know." Jennifer laughed happily. What fun! Ken stood beside her beaming proudly. After Colin in Alaska, he dialed in other ham operators around the country.

"Are those people really in those places?" she asked in awe. "Or do they live on the next block? How can a little radio like this reach so far?"

Ken smiled, his lively eyes filled with excitement. "Listen, hams talk all over the world, especially at night. The radio beams bounce off the ionosphere."

"The what?"

"It's just a layer of atmosphere. Because of the bounce, you can reach all sorts of places. Do you remember when the Columbia Space Shuttle went up? I could hear one of the astronauts, Owen Garriott. He's a ham, too. All the hams were listening to him."

Jennifer paused to look at him. What an amazing person! "How long have you been doing this?" she asked.

"Oh, about three years now, since I was fifteen."

She walked around the large garage. It was a marvelous hideaway. Ken had hung pictures and decorations on the walls. On a shelf on one wall, she saw several tarnished trophies. Curious, she picked one

79

up. She read the inscription. "First Place, State Mile Run, Kenneth Stanley."

"Hey," she exclaimed. "I didn't know you were a runner."

"Used to be," said Ken rather abruptly. "Haven't run in a few years."

Fascinated, Jennifer looked at the neglected trophy again. "But, Ken, you were state champion!" She looked at the date on the cup. "Why, you must have been only fifteen."

"I was," said Ken.

"Why did you quit running?"

Ken was suddenly standing close to her. He drew her to him, his powerful arms holding her tightly. He gazed deeply into her eyes. His kiss was warm on her lips and she could feel him tremble as he held her. She hardly knew whether she was in the Stanley garage in Springfield or in Alaska . . .

Later they drove home slowly, not talking now. Ken's hand held hers on the car seat, clutching it tightly. When they were at her front door, he kissed her again, lingeringly, as though he never wanted to let her go. She hugged him to her.

"I had a wonderful time," she said.

"Me too," Ken replied, holding her hands.

"I really wondered about you at first, Ken. The way you acted whenever I asked about the icehouse."

"Jennifer, you don't understand," he said urgently. "Someone was killed at that place a few years ago."

"Killed?" Jennifer asked, shocked.

"Yes. It was just some kids exploring the place, but the boy was just as dead." He pulled her into his arms again. "Don't you see, Jenny? I couldn't stand it if something happened to you out there." Ken's kiss was gentle on her lips. "I'll call you tomorrow," he whispered. And then he was gone, hurrying down the walk to his car.

Sleep was almost impossible for Jennifer that night. Floating before her were Ken's dark eyes. They were such troubled eyes and she could not get rid of the feeling that he still had not told her everything.

Chapter 8

Leisurely reading the Sunday *Times* over coffee had become one of Jennifer's favorite weekend relaxations since she had joined the newspaper staff. Usually she devoured every page, loving the by-lines because now she knew the writers and editors. She savored every small contribution she had made, too, the captions and various additions she had made to stories for the feature sections. But this Sunday she restlessly leafed through the pages, reading hardly more than a sentence or two before her mind wandered. In her mind she still saw the troubled face of Ken Stanley. By noon she could stand it no longer. She walked outside to her Datsun and drove downtown to the *Times*.

The security guard at the door wasn't one she knew, but he motioned her through when she flashed her lime-green press identification card. Jennifer went to her desk in the entertainment department and got the envelope of clippings about the Stanley icehouse that Mike Fallon had given her. She could not wait until tomorrow to find out about the icehouse. Maybe the articles held a clue to what was bothering Ken Stanley. She sat at her desk in the deserted entertainment department and began reading.

These were not old stories, which, as Mike had told her, were probably on microfilm in the files. These were quite recent clippings. The first one, from three years ago, took Jennifer's breath away.

16-Year-Old Youth Dies Exploring Old Icehouse

A 16-year-old Springfield youth was killed yesterday when he fell from a catwalk outside the abandoned Stanley Icehouse at Miller Pond near Holly Hills.

The dead boy, Thomas Gallagher of 1274 North Hampton Avenue, was exploring the abandoned structure with Kenneth Stanley, 15, whose father owns the icehouse.

Jennifer felt the clipping fall from her fingers. Her hands were trembling. *"You don't understand,"* Ken had told her, *"someone was killed at that place three years ago . . ."* But he had not mentioned that the someone was a friend of his, or that he himself was there at the time! She picked up the clipping and read on. Dazed, she tried to concentrate on the terrible story.

Stanley had a key to the rotting old structure, which has been condemned and is awaiting demolition, and had taken his friend on an exploratory trip, police said.

Gallagher, a classmate of young Stanley at Washington High School, plunged almost 70 feet to his death.

No criminal charges were immediately filed against young Stanley. The matter has been turned over to Lincoln County Juvenile Court authorities.

Jennifer sat frozen at her desk, unable to move or think. No wonder the subject of the icehouse always drew such a reaction from Ken. What had happened inside the deserted old place that day? Whatever it was, why hadn't he told her the truth? Was he ashamed? Or even guilty? Was there something about Tom Gallagher's death that had not come out even yet? Was she putting herself in danger by asking Ken about the icehouse? At least she understood now why Ken had looked at her with such intensity when she asked him questions. He couldn't talk about it. He wanted to forget the whole thing.

Jennifer was so caught up in her thoughts that she didn't at first realize there was one more clipping. It was dated only a few weeks ago and the headline read:

Stanley & Co. Sued
In Icehouse Death

The story told of a lawsuit against Stanley & Company and Ken's father, Richard, by Tom Gallagher's parents, charging negligence in the death of their son. It said that after long legal negotiations, an out-of-court settlement would probably be completed soon. Jennifer shivered. That must have been the story Ken thought she was chasing when she first went to see him. That's why he had said, *"I've been instructed to say there will be no comment on the case."*

Jennifer shoved the clipping back into the envelope and threw it into her desk drawer. She was on her feet and hurrying out of the *Times* building almost before she knew it. She knew she had to get away; she had to get out of there! She dashed through the front lobby, past the security guard, and ran to her Datsun.

As she climbed into the little silver car and drove out of the parking lot, she realized she didn't have any place to go. She could *not* go home. Ken said he would call her today, and she wasn't sure she knew what to say to him. Actually, she might never know what to say to him again. So she headed the car west toward Holly Hills. When Wendy answered the door, Jennifer practically fell into her arms with relief. "Gosh, I'm glad you're home," she said. "I really needed a friendly, familiar face."

"What's the matter?" Wendy asked at once, looking

into Jennifer's troubled face. "You look as though you've lost your last friend."

"Oh, I hope not, Wendy! Because I need somebody to talk to." As her answer, Wendy led her unhappy friend to the porch swing and they both sat down.

"This day has been something else. You wouldn't believe it," Jennifer said, picking restlessly at the tassels on one of the swing pillows.

"What happened?" Wendy pressed her, looking concerned.

"You remember I've been telling you about dating Ken Stanley?"

"Yes. He took you to Royal Oaks, didn't he? He sounds fascinating." Wendy smiled.

"He is," Jennifer said, turning to face Wendy. "Maybe too fascinating."

"What do you mean, Jenny?"

"Ken told me last night that someone was killed in the old icehouse."

"Killed!"

"It was an accident, he said. But he didn't tell me everything. I went to the office today and read some stories about the icehouse from the *Times* library. It was a sixteen-year-old boy who was killed . . . and Ken Stanley was with him." The bare facts sounded awful spoken aloud.

"Jenny!" Wendy cried. "Was he arrested?"

"No. The story said no criminal charges were filed."

Wendy digested the information. "That doesn't sound the same as 'innocent' to me."

"It isn't, Wendy. I just feel so awful!"

"Good grief, Jenny! Are you telling me that you're dating someone you think might be guilty of . . ."

"I've asked myself that question a thousand times since I read those clippings," Jennifer said in anguish, getting up and pacing restlessly back and forth on the porch, "and I just don't have the answer."

A lot about Ken Stanley finally made sense to her now. She knew now why he had seemed so shy, so tormented at times. *"I haven't done much lately,"* he had told her. He had only been fifteen when his friend was killed. After that, he'd probably withdrawn into himself. It all swam around in her head. The hurt he must have suffered! No wonder he quit running track. He couldn't face people anymore, even if he was the state mile champ. He had retreated into his garage, into amateur radio, into talking with people in Alaska and Russia. Anywhere but Springfield!

And now she had stumbled upon his guilty secret.

"Do you think it's dangerous to be with him?" Wendy asked, her eyes filled with worry.

Jennifer sat on the steps, picked up a leaf, and shredded it nervously. "I don't know, Wendy. He seems so . . ."

"So what?"

"So . . . mixed up, Wendy. Sometimes there's so much pain in his eyes that I want to put my arms around him and comfort him. But other times . . ."

"What? Other times *what?*"

Jennifer shook her head in uncertainty. "It's hard to explain, but he seems about ready to explode."

Wendy sank down beside Jennifer on the steps and took her hands. "Listen, Jenny, be careful, will you?"

"I'll be careful," Jennifer replied evenly. "Thanks, Wendy."

"Listen, Jenny," Wendy said, trying to lighten up her friend's mood. "Why don't we fix something to eat and then catch the early movie at the Crescent Theater over in the mall?"

"Wendy, you're just what the doctor ordered. Let me call home and tell Mom."

"I'll check the fridge while you use the phone," Wendy said, opening the door. "Come on!"

As the girls munched on tacos and sipped the chocolate shakes Wendy had made, Jennifer felt some of the tension leaving her body. On the ride to the movie, they talked about everything except Ken Stanley.

Sitting in the dark theater, Jennifer felt better than she had in several days. "I owe you one, Wendy," she said softly.

But Jennifer couldn't escape her worries for long. As she hurried through the city news room the next afternoon, she heard assistant city editor Jack Markman talking on the phone.

"Taylor, it's Markman," the editor said. He was talking to the reporter who covered the courthouse news. "Listen, that Stanley case is up this afternoon before Judge McAllister. Check it out, okay?"

Jennifer's steps slowed. The settlement on the Gallagher case! Ken would be there. Oh, how she wanted to know what would happen. She thought for a moment. Kathleen had said she would be out all afternoon interviewing a visiting opera star. Jennifer had done most of her work already. If something extra hadn't come in for her to do, she could probably leave for an hour.

The Lincoln County Courthouse was only three blocks away from the *Times* building, in Courthouse Square. It took Jennifer only a few minutes to walk quickly to the imposing old building with its immense stone pillars and great, wide stone steps. She walked into the high-ceilinged main lobby and spotted an information booth.

"Excuse me," she asked a tiny gray-haired man who was seated on a stool in the booth, "can you please tell me where the Stanley case is being heard?"

"What's that?" the man said. "Stanley?"

"Yes, sir. It's about Tom Gallagher."

The man looked at a long sheet of paper in front of him and ran his fingers down a typed list of names. "Stanley . . . Gallagher . . . let's see here. Ah, *Gallagher vs. Stanley*. Judge McAllister's case. That's just down the hall to the left."

As Jennifer hurried along the corridor, she saw a group of people coming out of a courtroom. And then she saw Ken. He was walking with a beautiful, slim redheaded girl, and they were as close to each other as two people can possibly be. Jennifer stepped back against the wall, terrified of being seen. Suddenly the beautiful young redhead was in Ken's arms, holding

90

on to him frantically, weeping so hard that she shook. Ken held her, unmoving. Jennifer could see that he was crying, too.

Ashamed and embarrassed, Jennifer backed away down the hallway to the lobby, stumbled out of the courthouse onto those massive stone steps, and ran heedlessly down, hardly able to see through the tears in her eyes.

She wondered if she would ever see Ken again. She knew she would never feel the same about him.

Chapter 9

Jennifer had little recollection later of walking back to the *Times*. Her eyes were misty and her head ached. She hadn't imagined how much she could be hurt. She knew there was no longer any need to worry about choosing between Ken and Billy.

She hurried back into the entertainment department to have a last look before going home. Everything seemed all right. On her desk was a scrawled note from Billy, and just the sight of it made her feel better. It said simply, "Jenny, I stopped by to see you. Sorry I missed you, Pretty Face. I'll call tonight. Love, Billy."

The note cheered her up a little, but it was still a long drive home in the Datsun that evening. It struck her that she was adrift, that nothing was getting solved. She couldn't go on like this much longer.

Dinner that night seemed to take forever. Johnny

swirled his mashed potatoes around on his plate and tried to strike up a conversation about the Chicago White Sox, his favorite team. Mr. and Mrs. Taggert watched their daughter with concern, but realized she wanted to be alone with her thoughts. After dinner Jennifer sat restlessly before the television set, unable to concentrate on the screen. Twice, she checked the phone to make sure it was working. If only Billy would call. He had said he would. How she needed his funny jokes and charming compliments to cheer her up. At the same time, she was afraid that Ken might call, and what in the world could she say to him?

Finally the phone did ring. For once Johnny wasn't there to snatch it up. She let it ring several times. Ken or Billy? she wondered. But the voice on the end wasn't either of them. It was a call Jennifer wasn't expecting but had subconsciously known would come sooner or later.

"Hello?"

"Jennifer?" came a distraught voice. It was Kathleen Owens.

"This is Jennifer, Kathleen. Is anything wrong?" She knew something had to be wrong for Kathleen to call her at home.

"I'm afraid so," Kathleen managed in a voice that trembled. "There are albums missing from the cabinet. I discovered it when I got back to the office a half hour ago."

Jennifer's heart sank at the words. Of course, it was bound to happen. No matter how hard she had tried,

94

she had been unable to prevent it. "Which ones are gone, Kathleen?" she asked.

"Several, Jennifer. And the problem is, I've already promised Tom I'd review two of them this week. Do you have any explanation at all?"

"Did you check my list?" Jennifer asked, clutching at straws.

"Of course I checked the list," Kathleen said, her voice rising even higher. "You logged them in this morning."

"Kathleen, I don't know what to tell you," Jennifer said. How could she explain the unexplainable? There was a pause, and Jennifer could hear her boss puffing away nervously on a cigarette. "Did you take some albums home *again,* Jennifer?"

"No, no, Kathleen. I told you I've *never* taken any records home."

"Well, I'm sorry, Jennifer, but someone is going to have to explain this to Tom Whitney tomorrow morning!" The fear and panic in the woman's voice had suddenly been replaced by anger. "I told Tom I was going to review albums by the Stray Cats and Linda Ronstadt, and he is planning specific feature tie-ins. He is not going to be pleased at all."

"Kathleen," Jennifer interrupted, trying to placate her, "I don't blame you for being angry. I'm angry, too! I've wanted to tell you about this, but didn't know how."

"Tell me what?" Suspicion tinged Kathleen's every word.

"Somebody has been taking albums from the cabinet and then bringing them back later."

There was silence.

"It's been driving me crazy, and I don't pretend to understand it," Jennifer finally went on.

"Really!"

"It's true, Kathleen."

"Jennifer, we've been all through this. Only you and I have keys! *I* checked with the maintenance department about this, too, you know. One of the men told me you had gone down there. There are no other keys!" Kathleen's panic was only too real; she obviously wasn't trying to make Jennifer look bad. She was worried about her own job!

Jennifer felt lost.

"You report to me first thing in the morning, Jennifer. And you'd better have those records with you! This has gone on long enough. You'll have to talk to Tom Whitney. I simply cannot protect you any longer." And the phone went dead.

When Jennifer walked into the *Times* entertainment department the next morning, she thought to herself, *There's one last hope. If the bizarre pattern of the past holds, the two missing albums could be back in the locked file cabinet by now.*

She hurried to the cabinet, her hands trembling as she unlocked it. But she couldn't remember the exact titles of the albums, and before she could do a check against the index list, the solemn figure of Kathleen Owens marched in, her face paler than usual.

"Well," she said, pausing without even going to her desk, "did you get in here early again and return them?"

"No, Kathleen."

"Oh! You kept them?"

"No, no, no! I didn't take them, so I couldn't have returned them," Jennifer said as calmly as she could.

Kathleen walked to her desk, sat down slowly, her eyes never leaving Jennifer, and said challengingly, "All right, Jennifer. Bring me the Linda Ronstadt album. You told me she's one of your favorites. The album just came in yesterday. It's going to be a hot item, something you'd like to get in advance."

Jennifer felt a curious calm spreading through her. There was no sense in getting angry or upset. But she knew she had to solve the perplexing mystery this time or else lose her job. "I did not take the album," she said firmly.

"Then bring it to me."

Jennifer looked at her list for the title and then checked the cabinet with extra care. "It's not here."

"I thought not," Kathleen snapped impatiently. "Now bring me the new one by the Stray Cats."

Jennifer again checked the list and the cabinet. "Not here," she said levelly. "I told you last night, Kathleen. Something crazy has been going on. I wanted to tell you before, but I was afraid . . ."

"Of what?"

"That you'd think I took them."

"What else am I supposed to think?" she asked irritably. "I do not intend to be blamed for this! And I suppose you're going to pretend you don't come in here during off hours to *borrow* records."

The accusation stunned Jennifer. How could anyone think her capable of that kind of sneaky behavior? Outraged by Kathleen's assumption, she answered instantly. "I have never in my life done anything like that!"

"No?" Kathleen's sudden smile made Jennifer uneasy. "Will you come in for a moment, Harry?" she called over her shoulder.

Jennifer's heart sank as the husky man in a security guard uniform walked into the room. She recognized him as the one who had let her in last Sunday.

"Have you ever seen this young woman come into the office during off hours?" Kathleen asked with a smug smile.

"Yes, ma'am. I let her in just last Sunday afternoon."

"Kathleen, I can explain!" Jennifer burst out. It looked so incriminating, she realized. But she was *innocent!* "Kathleen, it's true I came in on Sunday, but not to take albums, I swear." She could hear the fear in her own voice. "I just came in to get something from my desk. You have to believe me!"

"I'm fresh out of belief, Jennifer," Kathleen said with a tired sigh. "But you're getting a brief reprieve. Tom is in Chicago, so I won't be able to talk to him until he gets back next Monday."

"What will you tell him, Kathleen?"

"The truth, Jennifer. That I no longer feel I can trust you to work with me."

Jennifer felt her face burning hot and her heart thumping. She hardly knew how she would get through the week.

When Wendy's invitation came, it seemed to Jennifer like a pardon from a life term in Sing Sing. "Why don't you come out and spend the weekend with me? Maybe a change of scenery would help," her friend suggested.

"I'd be rotten company," Jennifer warned.

"You don't have to act like company with us, Jenny. You don't even have to talk to anyone if you don't feel like it."

"In that case, you've got a visitor."

Jennifer couldn't think of a better escape. It was a place to hide, practically. Maybe she could think things out. Maybe there was an explanation for the increasingly weird things that were happening to her— because there was no longer any doubt in her mind that somebody was manipulating her and Kathleen, too, for some reason. But why? And how?

Sunday was a truly glorious summer day at the Jamison farm. But when Wendy and her father invited Jennifer to go riding with them, she declined at the last moment.

"No. You two go ahead," Jennifer replied. "I need some time alone to think."

"All right, but don't think *too* hard," Wendy said, scrambling to her feet as her father appeared, dressed for riding.

Wendy and her father walked off the porch and around to the corral. Jennifer could see them saddling the two horses, and then riding across the meadow in the direction of the old quarry. She sat there, trying to relax in the comfortable old front porch swing. But her mind kept returning to the mystery of what was going on at the *Times*. She had gone over it at least a thousand times before. Why would somebody take review albums and then bring them back later? And how would they do it? Of course, she was often gone for hours at a time running errands and helping out on projects for other editors in the department. And the office was so big, and the staff so busy, that it would be possible, Jennifer realized, for someone to sneak the albums out in the middle of the day—provided no one was around.

But they had to have a key! Was there someone at the paper who wanted to cause her grief? Someone who wanted her fired? Did she have an unknown enemy there? That just couldn't be. Stop it, she told herself. Think of something else.

Ken Stanley slid into her mind. He was an uncertain topic, as well. She hadn't told Wendy that Ken didn't just happen to be in the old icehouse with the Gallagher boy. He'd had the key. He had led the way. And she had said nothing about the beautiful redhead he had embraced at the courthouse. Well, she didn't want to think about all that, either.

Restlessly she got up from the swing and walked aimlessly around the long, wide porch. Almost without making the decision, she found herself walking out past the corral and across the field. The day was warm and lovely, with a few lazy white clouds floating along overhead. It was a day designed to banish troubles. She walked on. Soon she realized she was going in the direction of the icehouse. That was perfect. She would forget everything else and have another look at the old place.

Chapter 10

Walking steadily, Jennifer crossed the grassy field, stepping on rocks to cross the stream at the bottom of the valley. By then she was following the rusty railroad tracks. And there it was.

Somehow, the sprawling, paint-chipped old pile of bricks and rotting platforms seemed even more ominous than the first time she had seen it. Maybe it was because now she knew Tom Gallagher had died there. Maybe it was because of Ken Stanley's warning.

But she still thought it would make a good feature story. The place certainly had an interesting past.

Possible openings for such a story popped into her head. "The crumbling Stanley Icehouse on Miller Pond on the outskirts of Springfield is a relic of the city's past, when life was simple and—some people say—better." If she could write a story like that, maybe it would even help her escape from the entertainment department and its headaches.

Jennifer walked closer. Carefully she climbed onto the platform that held the rotting wooden office. She wiped away a thick layer of dirt from one of the windows and peered in. She could make out a small wooden desk and a broken chair. She circled around, looking at the metal doors set into the brick building. The ice must have slid out of those doors onto the platform, and then been loaded into trucks and wagons and freight cars. On one door was a sturdy-looking padlock and the huge unavoidable sign:

DANGER!
THIS PROPERTY IS CONDEMNED!
TRESPASSERS WILL BE PROSECUTED!

The brick walls, once painted green, had faded to a dirty, muddy color, Jennifer noticed as she walked around the building. Wild, untamed grass grew between the rusty railroad tracks and sprouted between cracks in the foundation. In the rear wall she discovered another old wooden door, but it too was padlocked and posted as "Condemned." Another rusty set of tracks ran beside the wall there. Old metal ice chutes eight feet long were piled on end, leaning against the wall. The chutes apparently had carried blocks of ice across the platform and into trucks or railroad cars.

Then she noticed something under the chutes, a square inset in the wall, a small rusty door about four feet high by four feet wide. Years ago, three-hundred-pound blocks of ice must have slid through that small door and out through the chutes. Jennifer kneeled down and peeked under the ice chutes. She reached her hand to the iron door in the wall and shoved it.

The door gave under her weight!

Jennifer felt her heart thump. The door, apparently on a spring mechanism, opened when you pushed it. When you stopped pushing, it clanged back in place. At last she'd found a way inside. By now burning with curiosity, Jennifer pushed on the little iron door. She stuck her head inside and peered into the dark, cavernous void. Muted shafts of light from somewhere showed a solid floor just inside. She took a breath and pushed the door back, climbing into the icehouse.

Jennifer stood up. There was only enough light from the filthy windows for her to see that she was in a corridor that ran along the icehouse from one end to the other. Beyond that wall, she thought, must be the big room where ice was stored. There was a metal conveyor belt in the corridor's floor which once moved ice blocks along. A musty, rotting smell assailed her nose, and there was a faint smell of ammonia.

Jennifer edged along the corridor toward the middle of the icehouse, stepping cautiously along, following the conveyor belt, which was set in a groove in the floor with iron teeth sticking up.

After she had gone a short distance, she heard something. She froze and listened. Maybe she was imagining things.

She heard it again. A swift scurrying. She was not alone in the icehouse!

Jennifer read herself off for an idiot! She stood rooted to the spot, frozen in terror.

Again! Swift scampering. A curious, high-pitched cry. And then, in a patch of light on the floor, she saw it, scurrying frantically across the conveyor belt just in front of her and darting into a jagged hole.

A rat with red, furtive eyes.

Jennifer stifled a scream. Terrifying as it was, she was glad it was only a rat, and obviously more afraid of her than she was of it. She let out a breath. Gradually, the layout of the interior began to make sense to her. The icehouse was like a house within a house. The corridor ran around the edge, separating the big central storage room from the outer wall. The workers moved around this outer corridor, shifting blocks of ice onto the conveyor chain, which then carried them to the chutes in the outer wall.

Then Jennifer saw a door leading from the outer corridor into the central ice storage room. She tried it and it opened grudgingly, squeaking and sagging. She peered into the foggy gloom, the only light coming from a small skylight in the ceiling. A large room opened before her, the floor littered with abandoned chutes, tongs, and bulky shapes covered with tarpaulins. Her heart in her mouth, Jennifer stepped through the door. *Get out of here,* an inner voice screamed at her. But it was absolutely fascinating!

She took another step into the gloom, then another. It was as though she were in the middle of an immense underground cavern or some old forgotten cathedral. The room was enormous! It rose straight up for seven stories, stretching across the better part of a block in one direction, and half that in the other.

Enthralled, her heart beating wildly, Jennifer squinted upward to the distant ceiling. And then, as though in a nightmare, she imagined something hurtling from the very top of the building and plunging to the floor. That's what had happened to Tom Gallagher in this terrifying, abandoned deathtrap.

Jennifer shivered at her own overactive imagination. Suddenly a sound startled her. Rats! she thought. But then she realized it was coming from beyond the thick wall. Somebody else *was* in the icehouse! She could hear muffled voices, and they were approaching the door to the ice storage room!

It must be the demolition crew, she decided hurriedly. If she were caught trespassing, she could be prosecuted! She dreaded to think what her parents would say if she were to become their next legal client. She looked around wildly for a hiding place. Near the door were black plastic tarps thrown over something. But that was too close.

There was no way out now without running into the demolition crew. Jennifer hurried deeper into the vast room, away from the door, dodging behind piles of oily railroad ties and a huge piece of machinery. Thank goodness she had worn sneakers! She crouched behind a stack of rusty ice chutes far from the door, wrapping her arms around her legs, pulling her knees up under her chin. She burrowed deeper under the ice chutes. *Don't let them find me!* she prayed, making herself as small as possible while the voices drew closer.

Voices floated across the great room to her, but she couldn't make out words. And then she heard music. They had brought along a box radio to entertain them while working, she realized. If they were playing music, how long might they stay? *Why didn't I listen to Ken?* she thought miserably. Her curiosity had gotten her into trouble before, but not to this extent. Her mind was in a turmoil. *I should just stand up and say, "Hi! I wanted to see what the place looked like, so I decided to explore." What could they do to me?*

She was about to come out of her hiding place and chance it when she caught some barely audible words: ". . . she won't be trouble much longer . . . stop worrying . . ." The voice was unclear, and she was tired and cold, but Jennifer knew instinctively that it wasn't the right time to stand up and introduce herself.

The music began again. It sounded like some rock stuff she'd heard before, but she couldn't identify it because of the echoes and distortion. Why didn't the demolition team just do their work and get out? Her back hurt and her arms were beginning to throb; she was longing to escape from behind the ice chutes. Why did they keep turning the radio off and on? They were acting pretty strange for demolition experts.

Finally she heard more fragments of conversation.

". . . fixing her up good . . . won't even know what happened to her . . ." They were still talking about some woman. But they didn't sound very friendly.

Then there was a snatch of music. More wild, howling rock, which was abruptly cut off.

The men stayed on and on, and every second was utter misery for Jennifer. The concrete floor was so cold, her whole body was sore, and she was certain she'd never get the splinters out of her hands. The time dragged endlessly. Would they never leave?

Despite the discomfort, Jennifer dozed off. The sound of a door banging shut woke her. Startled, she looked at her watch. Two and a half hours had passed.

But was it safe to come out yet? As much as she wanted to stand up and stretch, she decided to stay in hiding another five minutes, just in case they came back.

When she finally stood up, her muscles screamed in protest. "One more minute behind those chutes and I'd have to be carried out of here on a stretcher," she muttered, moving awkwardly across the floor, guided by the fading rays from the skylight. She looked around the room again. Why had those men stayed in here for two and a half hours? Nothing seemed different about the room. There were no signs of wires or explosives, thank goodness! That would be all she needed. She could even envision the headline: "Nosy Copyperson's Big Story Blows Up In Her Face!"

Then something to the right of the door caught her eye. A wire. Maybe they had been rigging up the place for destruction. A cold shiver of fear flashed through her. She inched closer to the wire. It was black and led to the bulky tarp-covered objects she had noticed earlier. Jennifer stretched out her hand to the corner of the tarp. What would be the harm in taking a quick look?

She pulled aside the plastic, her eyes widening in amazement. The tarp had been covering a stereo set! What in the world was a stereo doing in an abandoned icehouse? So that's where the music was coming from. They must have used a generator to supply power to it. But none of it made sense to Jennifer's logical mind. Why bother dragging a stereo and generator out here? Nobody was screwy enough to come out here just to listen to music!

Mystified, she began pulling other tarps off, exposing enough state-of-the-art stereos and tape decks to stock a small appliance store. Gasping with surprise and excitement, Jennifer ran to another pile and threw back the tarps. Video-cassette recorders! And they were all hooked together with a complicated maze of wires.

Think, Jennifer! It's your arms and legs that are cramped, not your brain. "Of course!" she shouted, her voice echoing in the vast room. Hadn't she been reading about the rash of burglaries in Springfield? She was surrounded by stolen goods! She had stumbled upon a burglary ring. Thank heavens she had not stood up and said, "Hi!"

Quickly she covered up the stolen stereos, tape decks, and VCRs and left the icehouse the way she had entered. Hurrying back through the high grass toward Wendy's, she realized she had a real "hard news" story now—not just a feature about an old icehouse.

It wasn't until she was safely back inside Wendy's house that the ugly thought intruded upon her. A burglary ring was using the Stanley icehouse, and Ken Stanley had continually warned her to stay away from the place!

Was it possible? Could Ken Stanley, who had been mixed up in the death of Tom Gallagher, be involved with a burglary ring? Images of his dark, troubled eyes swam before Jennifer, and suddenly she felt cold with fear.

Chapter 11

Later that afternoon, when Jennifer was driving back from Holly Hills to the city, her mind was in turmoil. Was Ken Stanley leading a burglary gang and using the old icehouse to store stolen goods? It was mind-boggling! Was it his voice she had heard echoing through the storage room? Was that Ken Stanley saying, *"she won't be trouble much longer,"* and did "she" mean *Jennifer?*

Ceaselessly, in her mind she replayed her conversations with Ken. *Don't go near the icehouse,* he kept telling her. He certainly hadn't told her the whole truth about Tom Gallagher's death. And those sudden, frightening outbursts of rage when he would snap, "I know what you're after!" She was beginning to feel she had wasted time and energy feeling sorry for him.

You must go to the police, she told herself. And then

she thought, *Wow, what a story this will make! I'll really be able to get something into the* Springfield Times! *Maybe,* she fantasized, *I can do a story under my own by-line.* Glorious possibilities sprang up in her imagination:

Young Reporter Cracks
Icehouse Burglary Gang
By Jennifer Taggert

But just as swiftly, she realized that if she went to the police or told the city news editor about the story, it wouldn't be hers for long. No, she needed to get the facts really nailed down first, so they couldn't take it away from her. No one knew about her discovery, not even those burglars.

By the time she turned off onto Webster Avenue, she had decided to wait until the next day. She would talk to somebody who could help. *Pictures,* she thought, *I need photographs!* She would go back out to the icehouse with a camera and get proof on film of all those stolen stereos, tape decks, and videocassette recorders. Then she could lay it all before the city editor and the police!

After an endless night during which she hardly slept, Jennifer was at the *Times* early next morning. The first person she ran into was a scowling Kathleen Owens. Jennifer had almost forgotten her troubles over the albums because of her excitement over the icehouse story. But obviously the missing review records were still uppermost in Kathleen's mind.

"Jennifer," she said right away, "I've set up a meeting with Tom Whitney for ten A.M. tomorrow. Be there."

There was no need to ask what it would be about. "Yes, Kathleen," Jennifer sighed.

The usual scrambling work routine swallowed her up for several hours after that, and she had little time to even think about the icehouse. It wasn't until she brought coffee to Joe Davis, the science writer, that she thought again of something that had been puzzling her.

"Joe," she began, handing him his coffee, "have you ever written anything about stereos and videocassette recorders?"

"In my day, I've written about everything from noises to noses," he laughed.

"Have you ever heard of stereos wired together in a line, or VCRs all wired together?"

"Well, I suppose you might do that if you wanted to record a few tapes all at one time."

Jennifer pondered that. "You mean, you could play something on one set and it would play on the others, too."

"Yes, that's the way it works. Why?"

Maybe the burglars had been testing the stereos to make sure they all were in working order. "I don't know exactly," said Jennifer. "Would that be difficult, wiring things up like that?"

"No, not for anybody who knows electronics."

Then an idea came to Jennifer in a flash. "How about somebody who has a ham radio set?"

"Sure," said Davis. "That kind of wiring would be a piece of cake for a ham radio operator."

Jennifer walked away, her excitement growing. It was all falling into place. Now all she needed was proof!

And when Billy Singleton strolled up to her desk just before lunch and invited her out for a bite to eat, she knew she had found the person to help her. As they walked over to the Lantern, they chatted about the usual things, but as soon as they were seated at the restaurant, Jennifer couldn't wait to tell her story. "Billy, you're not going to believe this!" Through quick bites of her cheeseburger, Jennifer poured out her story of the stolen goods at the icehouse and her suspicions about Ken Stanley.

Billy listened, his eyes wide with amazement. "Jenny, you've got yourself some story," he declared when she was done.

"I know! But can I hold on to it? I've got to go back out there and take some pictures."

Billy reacted sharply to that. "Wait a minute, Scoop," he protested. "You're not dealing with the Kennel Club Show here. You're not going out there alone. You don't know what might happen. I'm going with you."

"Would you really?"

"You bet I would," he answered. "Look, I've got a great camera. Right after work, I'll drive you out there. Pretty Face, I think you must be a born reporter." Billy's smile made Jennifer blush with pride.

When she returned to her desk after lunch, there

was a message for her: "Ken Stanley called. Wants you to call back." There was no way she could talk to him. She crumpled the paper and threw it into the wastebasket.

Billy's Mustang was waiting in front of the *Times* when Jennifer came hurrying out after work. She climbed in, exclaiming, "Billy, the stuff in that warehouse is unbelievable. They've got a regular appliance store out there."

The drive out to Holly Hills took barely twenty minutes. Billy circled around, following Jennifer's directions as they tried to find a road leading to Miller Pond. When they crossed a set of rusty railroad tracks leading off into a vacant expanse overgrown with grass and weeds, Jennifer pointed. "Those tracks," she said. "They must lead to the icehouse. It's got to be back there someplace."

Billy looked at the overgrown field and shook his head uncertainly. "Well . . . if you say so."

He turned the car and headed through the high grass, moving along slowly and bumpily beside the railroad tracks. Twice he stopped and looked inquiringly at her. "Jenny, are you sure it's this way?"

"Yes, Billy, it has to be. I came in from the other side, but these are definitely the same tracks. Keep going."

Billy's Mustang bumped and jostled through the high grass, thumping in and out of ruts and holes. But finally the grass parted and there it was. Across the clearing stood the icehouse.

Billy gave a little whistle of amazement.

"Drive on," Jennifer directed. "We can park the car behind those trees so that no one will notice."

Once they had hidden the car, Jennifer led Billy to the iron door under the rusty ice chutes. She and Billy squeezed past the chutes and then through the iron spring door. They moved along the corridor where the iron-toothed conveyor belt stuck up in the floor. And at last they reached the entrance to the inner storage room. "You're not going to believe all the stuff they've got," Jennifer told him excitedly, opening the door and leading him into the foggy void of the huge room. But it was Jennifer who couldn't believe what she saw. There was nothing there!

Jennifer blinked. The rows of tape decks covered with black tarps were gone! There were no VCRs, no wires, nothing! All she could see were the old railroad ties and rusted machinery deeper in the old deserted room.

"Where are they?" Billy asked eagerly. "Back further someplace?"

Jennifer was speechless for a moment. Then she gestured helplessly at the space where the stolen goods had been. "Right . . . here . . . !"

"Where?"

"They're gone!" Billy glanced around the deserted floor, then looked up at her skeptically. "They were right here," Jennifer insisted. "What could have happened to them?"

"Are you sure this is the same place?"

Jennifer felt helpless frustration rise in her. "Oh, of

course this is the same place," she cried. "I don't understand."

Billy's voice was sympathetic. "Maybe they saw you and moved it all out," he suggested.

Maybe that was it. It had to be it. "But how could they have spotted me?" she asked. *Unless someone knows about your interest in this place,* her inner voice said. Was someone following her? Was that person Ken? Suddenly she hated the icehouse and the burglars. She hated Ken Stanley and the hurt he had brought.

"I wish I had never laid eyes on this place!" Jennifer cried.

"Too bad," Billy comforted her. "If they saw you, they'll probably never come back *here* again."

Jennifer turned around and walked out the door of the storage room. "I'm never coming back here either," she vowed.

Jennifer felt awful. Not only did she not have a story, but she had to face Tom Whitney the next morning. There seemed to be no way things could get worse. But she was wrong.

As she and Billy walked back around the icehouse toward the car, she saw someone standing nearby. "Billy!" she breathed, leaning back against him.

It was Ken Stanley, and he was glaring at her and Billy with eyes filled with anger. He stood there stiffly, his hands balled into fists at his sides, glowering at them. "Ken, what . . ." Jennifer began, her mouth suddenly dry.

"Didn't I tell you to stay away from here?" he shouted angrily. "Didn't I warn you that this place is dangerous?"

"Yes, but . . ."

"But you just couldn't resist snooping around," Ken said with heavy sarcasm. "Why do you want to rake up the past? Hasn't everyone suffered enough?"

Frightened by the force of his anger, Jennifer was temporarily at a loss for words. Thank goodness she wasn't alone. She glanced at Billy, who also seemed surprised by Ken's strange behavior.

"Hey, just a minute, fella," Billy said. "You don't have the right to speak to Jennifer in that tone of voice!" He seemed to be just as angry as Ken. He stepped away from Jennifer's side and stopped about three feet in front of Ken, and his hands tightened into fists, too.

The possibility of a fight catapulted Jennifer into action. She couldn't let Billy get hurt because of her! Stepping quickly between the two tense figures, she put her hand lightly on Billy's chest. "Billy, maybe we'd better leave," she suggested, still trying to push him away from Ken.

"Who are you?" Billy asked, still glaring at Ken and ignoring Jennifer's efforts at peacemaking. He cocked his fist in a menacing way. Jennifer was appalled. Was this the smiling, charming Billy Singleton who could make her laugh, who could make her melt with a look or a kiss?

"Who are *you?*" Ken shot back, raising his fist.

"This is absolutely ridiculous!" Jennifer shouted.

She was now just as angry as they were. Why in the world did boys think they could settle arguments with their fists? she wondered. "Ken Stanley, this is Billy Singleton and don't you dare start throwing punches!" She had their full attention now. They both stared at her in surprise, taking in the angry sparks shooting out of her brown eyes. "I don't know why you're so upset, Ken," she went on hastily. "Billy and I were just looking around. We certainly weren't going to damage your precious icehouse!" She looked at him innocently, pretending she didn't know a thing about the stolen goods.

"I don't care why you're here," Ken said harshly. "This is my family's property and I want you both off now!"

"Yeah? You and who else?" Billy shouted threateningly.

"I can and I *will* have you arrested for trespassing," Ken retorted, taking a step closer to them. "As a matter of fact, I can call the police on the CB radio in my car. They'll be here in minutes."

Billy paled a little as he put his hand on Jennifer's arm. "C'mon, Jenny," he said, pulling her toward his car. "Let's get out of here before this jerk gets us mixed up in something."

"And don't come back!" Ken shouted as Billy drove his car away slowly along the railroad tracks.

Chapter 12

"Do you actually know that guy?" Billy asked, after they had reached the paved road heading back toward Springfield.

Jennifer didn't answer immediately. She had gone out with Ken. She had talked with him, danced with him, even kissed him. But did she really know him? "I don't guess I do," she said slowly. She wondered why that should bother her, but it did.

"That's good, Jenny, because he looks like someone you should avoid." Billy reached over and gave her hand a reassuring squeeze. "You know, he just might be involved with those stereos and tape decks you told me about."

"That's the conclusion I've come to, Billy."

"I think you're absolutely right. It has to be him. It's his family place, right? And I heard him say he'd told you to stay away from it. The evidence seems overwhelming."

"It's up to me to do something about it," Jennifer said decisively.

"What are you talking about, Jenny? What can you do?" Billy glanced at her, puzzlement and concern in his expression.

"I'll go to the police. I'll tell them what I saw in the icehouse yesterday." Now that she had made up her mind, Jennifer was anxious to get back into town. "Let's drive directly to the police station, Billy."

"The police? Hey, hold on a minute, Jenny." Billy eased up on the accelerator and brought the car to a stop on the shoulder of the road. He placed his hands on her arms and shook her gently. "Don't you know you could get into trouble doing that?"

"How could telling the truth get me into trouble?"

"You don't have any proof, Jenny. There are no tape decks there now. The cops would only laugh at you. And if you brought Stanley's name into it you could get sued for slander."

Jennifer sighed. "You're right, of course, Billy," she conceded.

"Your best bet is to stay away from Stanley *and* that rotting old building," he advised, pulling the car back onto the road.

"Please take me back to my car so I can go home, Billy. I suddenly want this day to be over," she said, feeling tired and confused.

The next morning, when Jennifer awakened after a restless night, things looked no better. In fact, they looked a good deal worse. Her story about the ice-house had evaporated before her eyes. And she still had to face Tom Whitney to explain about the missing albums—despite the fact that she had no explanation ready. Her only hope was Tom's understanding. He couldn't possibly think her guilty of stealing or lying.

There was no bounce to Jennifer's step as she walked into the *Times* building, no smile for the security guard. All her thoughts were on the coming confrontation. She entered the entertainment department slowly, immediately aware of the tension in the air.

Kathleen Owens glanced up at her quickly, and then turned away. Kathleen looked so nervous, it almost seemed like she was the one in trouble. She lit a cigarette and walked over to Jennifer's desk. "Are you ready to see Tom?"

Jennifer didn't have to answer because just then Tom Whitney walked into the department. He strolled up to Jennifer's desk.

"Morning, Tom," said Kathleen nervously.

"Morning," said Tom, avoiding Jennifer's eyes. "Well?" he asked. "Did the albums show up?"

Kathleen shook her head, and peeked at Jennifer. "Jennifer says she doesn't know where they are."

"Is that true, Jennifer?" The entertainment editor fixed her with a steady gaze. There was no hint of friendly joking now. This was clearly business. "You have no idea what happened to those missing review albums?"

"No, sir," said Jennifer, feeling helpless, "but I'll

check the file again." She walked over to the cabinet and opened it, but there was no sign of the records. She shook her head forlornly. "Not here," she said.

"Okay," said Tom, gesturing to Kathleen. "Open her desk."

"Open my desk?" Jennifer gasped, astounded at the suggestion.

"It's the only place we haven't looked," said Tom. "I told Kathleen we'd open it this morning with all of us present."

Kathleen opened the drawer of the desk Jennifer had been using. If Jennifer hadn't been so flabbergasted, she would have fainted at that moment. There in the top drawer were the missing albums!

"What in the world . . . ?" Jennifer heard herself gasp.

Tom Whitney was looking at her sadly and shaking his head. "Jennifer . . . why?"

"Tom . . ." She couldn't finish.

"Jennifer," said Tom, "don't you have an explanation for this? I want to be fair."

Jennifer felt frozen, immobilized. "I can't explain it," she finally said.

"Why don't you take the rest of the day off?" Tom said. "Come and talk to me tomorrow." He started toward his office, then turned. "I'm very sorry, Jennifer."

"Me, too," she managed.

Jennifer was amazed. This couldn't be happening. She looked into Tom's face, which was a mixture of disappointment and embarrassment. But even as the confusion spread through her, another emotion was building inside Jennifer—overwhelming anger at whoever had done this to her.

Because this had been no accident, no haphazard set of coincidences that caused her to look guilty. The albums had been planted in her desk! From the beginning, a knowing hand had been at work, setting her up.

She couldn't really blame Tom or Kathleen. They were victims of this mysterious hoax as much as she was, although they didn't realize it. How could they, when Jennifer herself could not unravel it? There would have been no point in pleading with Tom. She had lost his trust, and no amount of begging would restore it. Only one thing could do that—proof of her innocence. Jennifer walked out of the *Times* in a daze, hardly aware of her actions. She hurried down the front steps without looking back, and drove glumly home.

Who would do this to me, who? she asked herself again and again. It has to be someone close to me, someone who knows my exact schedule. Someone who has a key to the cabinet. And, she told herself, there has to be a logical reason for all this. No one would have arranged such an elaborate scheme without a good reason. And that's where Jennifer ran into a brick wall.

What did anyone possibly have to gain by discrediting her and getting her out of the *Times?*

She was still turning ideas over in her mind when

she reached her house, turning into the driveway. She didn't see the other car at first, noticing it only when she heard her name being called. "Jennifer!" Parked at the curb was Ken Stanley's Thunderbird.

Involuntarily, she quickened her steps up the walk to the front door.

"Jennifer!" Ken was out of his car and running after her. He caught her as she reached the steps to the porch, grabbing her arm and turning her to face him. Jennifer's expression was such a mixture of suspicion and wariness that Ken dropped her arm and looked at her in surprise. "Are you all right?" he asked, seemingly concerned and yet showing an undercurrent of annoyance.

"What do you want?"

"Why are you looking at me like that?" he protested. "Are you sick?"

"I'm a lot of things right now, but sick isn't one of them."

"You're not making any sense, Jenny. What's the matter?"

Jennifer willed herself to be calm. "I asked what you were doing here, Ken."

"I called you at the office. Somebody told me you had gone home for the day. I assumed you were sick."

"I came home because I'm on the verge of being fired."

Ken's eyes widened. "What?"

Jennifer sank down on the steps, fighting off an impulse to cry. "Somebody set me up. Somebody wants me out of the *Times*."

"But why?" Ken was saying, sitting down beside her.

"That's what I have got to find out," she said levelly, staring directly into his eyes. "Do you have any ideas?"

"Me?" Ken appeared stunned by the question. "How could I?"

"I don't know, Ken. Strange things have been happening. And now you show up supposedly concerned about my health, but acting annoyed at the same time. Why?"

Ken looked away and a flush rose in his face. He looked at his shoes. "I'm afraid you'll be angry," he said softly.

"I'm already angry, Ken. Tell me!"

He took a deep breath, then slowly let it out. "Because I was just about half-crazy seeing you with another guy!"

"You mean Billy?"

Ken nodded his head. Then he glared at her. "And at the icehouse, too. In spite of what I told you, you still went out there!"

"Why didn't you want me to go there, Ken? Tell me the real reason."

"I already have. It's dangerous! A boy . . ."

"Tom Gallagher."

Ken's mouth opened and closed. He looked away. "I knew you'd find out."

"I have to know, Ken. Were you responsible in some way?"

Ken's face paled at her question. He put his hand

over his eyes and shook his head. "No," he whispered.

Jennifer wanted to reach out to him, but she couldn't. There were so many unanswered questions. "Ken, I don't mean to pry, but . . ."

"But what?" He didn't look up.

"There are things about that icehouse . . ."

Ken's hand fell away. He raised his eyes to meet hers. "I was fifteen, Jenny. Tom was a year older. It was his idea. The stories said I was leading the exploration, but I wasn't. Tom got one of my father's employees, Leonard Randolph, to make us a key for the place and then talked me into going out there."

"But the Gallaghers sued you."

"They had to, Jenny. It was an insurance matter. We're still friends with the Gallaghers. We were all at court the other day when it was settled. It raked up a lot of painful memories. Becky, Tom's sister, was in tears."

The image of that beautiful redhead in Ken's arms swam before her. She was Tom Gallagher's sister? "Yes, I know," she said. "I was there."

Confusion, then anger, spread over Ken's face. "You were *there?* Why? Another *story* to drag it all up again!"

"Ken, I . . . no, I wasn't there on a story," she protested. "I'm not really sure why I was there. Oh, Ken," she cried in frustration, "there are so many things I want to ask you, but . . . but, Ken, sometimes . . . sometimes I'm afraid of you!"

Ken turned away abruptly and paced restlessly back and forth along the walk. He ran his fingers through his hair, and finally looked back at her, his eyes reflecting hurt and bewilderment. And in that instant, Jennifer believed him. There was no way that Ken was responsible for Tom Gallagher's death.

Chapter 13

"For heaven's sake, Jennifer," Ken pleaded. "How can you be afraid of *me?* Don't you know how much I care about you!"

"Oh, Ken," Jennifer murmured, and in spite of herself, tears rolled down her cheeks. All the hurt and misery of the last week poured out of her. Her body shook and she covered her eyes. And then Ken was beside her, pulling her hands away from her face and trying to wipe away her tears. "Hey, Jenny, don't," he said softly. "Please don't!"

She looked up at him, tears still shimmering in her eyes. "I care about you, too, but I'm confused about you, Ken."

"Please," he begged, "ask me anything! Yes, I do feel guilty about Tommy, though it wasn't my fault. And because of that guilt, I quit running track and hid in my garage for three years. It took you to bring me out."

Jennifer looked at Ken tenderly for a moment. Then she shook herself, remembering what Joe Davis had said. "Ken," she said, "you're a ham radio operator. You know how to wire things . . . tape decks and VCRs . . ."

The sudden switch of the conversation brought a blank look to Ken's face. "Sure, why?"

And then Jennifer just blurted it out. "What were all those stolen tape decks doing inside the icehouse?"

"Stolen tape decks . . . ?"

"If you're mixed up in something, if somehow Tommy's death got you on the wrong track . . ."

A puzzled frown creased Ken's forehead as he listened intently. "Jenny, please believe me. I haven't the vaguest idea of what you're talking about."

Jennifer looked at him intently. Then, slowly and clearly, she recounted the whole story for him. She told him how she had gone inside the icehouse and found the burglary ring's stash of loot and how, when she returned with Billy, it was all gone.

"But that's crazy," he protested.

"Yes, it is, but it's all true. Something's going on. Now tell me, why were you out there when Billy and I came out of the icehouse?"

Ken sighed, a little embarrassed. "Well, Jenny, you know I . . . I like you a lot." He paused for a moment. "I really wanted to see you that day. But when I left a message at the *Times* for you to call me, you never did. So I decided to wait for you after work. Then I saw you getting into a car with another guy and . . . I know I shouldn't have, but . . . I followed you. I was so jealous. Then when I saw you were going to the icehouse, I thought you and that guy were out there to write that story . . . because the suit had just been settled. I was furious."

"You mean you really have no idea that burglars have been using the icehouse?"

"Absolutely not!" He stood up quickly. "I'm going out there right now and find out about this!"

Without even thinking of the possible danger, Jennifer declared, "I'm going with you!"

Driving out toward Miller Pond, Jennifer had a pang of worry. Could she still be wrong about Ken? If so, going to the icehouse with him alone could be the biggest—and maybe the last—mistake of her life. But there was no turning back now. She looked at him. He couldn't, he just couldn't be a thief.

Ken drove down an overgrown gravel road that led into the clearing around the old icehouse. She and Billy had not known about that road, and only a person familiar with the terrain would have been able to find it. As he drove, Ken was looking at the road. "There are recent tire tracks on this road," he said. "I noticed them the other day, but didn't think much about it. I figured it was just the demolition crew."

The car pulled into the clearing. Ken drove around behind the building and slid the car into a grove of trees. Together they walked up to the icehouse from the rear. "I got in through an iron spring door on the end," Jennifer said, starting to lead him that way.

"Never mind," said Ken, taking out a ring of keys. "My father owns the place, remember? I have keys."

Ken unlocked a rear door, one that Jennifer had tried on her first visit but had been unable to budge. They walked up a short, dark stairway and opened a door into the vast central storage room. "Hold on to me," said Ken, giving Jennifer his hand. He led her across the long, dimly lit storage room, past the piled-up railroad ties and rusted machinery. As they approached the door that Jennifer had used to get into the room before, they could make out the shapes of black tarps spread over bulky items. Slowly, Ken walked over and pulled the tarps off.

Jennifer gasped. The tape decks and VCRs were back!

Her first reaction was to run! She had blundered by coming out to this deserted place with Ken Stanley. He had lied again. There was the loot, and they were alone inside a dungeon surrounded by walls so thick that no one would hear her screams if he turned on her.

But Ken seemed totally uninterested in harming her. He was examining the stereos and VCRs with intense curiosity, looking at the way they were arranged and the wiring. "Would you look at this?" he was saying, amazed. "Multiplex wiring, an amplifying unit, a control panel!"

Calmer, Jennifer moved over beside him to look. "Would that let them check the equipment?" she asked.

Ken shook his head, trying to think it through. "No,

no, you don't need all those wires for that. They must have been making copies."

"Copies?" asked Jennifer.

"Yes. See, you can play a record on one stereo and make copies on each of these other machines." He noticed a pile of tape cassettes and picked one up. "Sure," he exclaimed, getting excited. "Each tape deck would make a cassette. And look! Here's a portable generator. It would give them all the power they need for this operation!"

Jennifer counted the number of tape decks that were wired together. "Three . . . six . . . twelve! You mean they could make twelve tapes by playing a record one time?"

"Absolutely," said Ken.

Jennifer suddenly remembered the music she had heard when she was hiding under the ice chutes. That was no radio rock station she had heard. It was a stereo playing while thieves made copies. And then the realization of what it meant struck her. "Record pirates!"

"What?" asked Ken.

"They've been making counterfeit copies of records and then selling them!"

Ken was already examining the VCRs. "They were making copies of films too," he said. "These machines are all wired up so they could play a movie and make a dozen copies."

"They aren't ordinary burglars," Jennifer said. "They're record and movie pirates."

"Look," Ken said, picking up a record which was

137

leaning against the stereo. "Here's an album they were copying."

Jennifer took it from him, and almost dropped it in shock. "But this album is from the *Times!*" she gasped. "It came out of my locked cabinet!"

"Are you sure?"

"Yes, I'm sure! See this little number on the corner of the album jacket. *I* put that there!"

What did it mean? she wondered dizzily. Here were the people who had been stealing records from her? Whoever they were, they'd been taking review albums from her cabinet, bringing them out to the icehouse to make copies, and then returning them.

"Ken," she blurted out, "these are the people who were trying to get me fired! Why, they're copying and selling the latest albums before they are even available in the stores."

Relief of a sort flooded through Jennifer. At last, there was an explanation for the disappearing records. She wasn't imagining things. It was all very clever actually. They'd steal a review album, make copies, and then return it. By the time Kathleen's column was printed, the pirates would already be selling tapes to stores! But . . . who? Jennifer thought.

"Shhh!" Ken grabbed her arm. "Somebody's coming."

Jennifer stood stock still. Through the thick walls she heard a dull metallic thud. The door to the icehouse was being opened.

"Get out of sight!" Ken whispered urgently, throwing tarps back over the recording equipment.

"We've got to hide!" she said frantically, pulling him toward the machinery where she had hidden two days ago.

Moments later, as they crouched behind the rusty ice chutes, they could hear footsteps and the door opening. Jennifer swallowed nervously, wondering if she was in for another agonizing two-hour wait. Muffled voices reached them and they both strained to make out the words. Ken pointed to another stack of chutes nearer the door. "Okay?" he mouthed. She nodded. Obviously, he was hoping to get close enough to hear what they were saying. They crept slowly on hands and knees, Jennifer's full skirt hampering her every move. The knees of her panty hose were being shredded by the rough concrete floor.

Then Jennifer heard a familiar voice say, "I told you it'd be safe to come back here. Have I ever steered you wrong?"

She turned to Ken, her eyes wide with disbelief. "Billy," she mouthed. But how could it be? He was her friend. He couldn't be a criminal. Somebody must have forced him into doing this, she was certain.

"Don't get cocky, kid," an older voice snarled. "We almost got caught the other day by that snoopy girl." Snoopy girl! That meant her.

Ken tapped her on the shoulder. "Randolph," he mouthed. She peeked around the end of the stack of chutes and saw a heavyset man in a rumpled brown suit. It was the man who had tried to steal her purse.

"I took care of that, didn't I?" Billy said. "As a

139

matter of fact, I had that little nuisance in the palm of my hand right from the first," he boasted.

"Yeah, lover boy, you really have a way with the ladies," Randolph sneered.

"I guess I shouldn't take too much credit in her case," Billy said harshly. "She was a pushover." He laughed.

The shock and confusion Jennifer had felt a few minutes before was being rapidly replaced by anger. No, it went beyond anger. For the first time in her life, she understood what was meant by white-hot rage.

"I still say you should have dropped her as soon as we got her key copied," Randolph insisted.

It was all becoming horribly clear to Jennifer. Billy! He'd had a copy made of her key that first night at the Cave. He'd been friendly to her so he could steal records from the entertainment department. And then she had even told him about the tape decks, so he could move them all out of the icehouse! What a fool she had been!

"You're wrong, Len," Billy was saying. "If I hadn't conned that dumb high school kid into thinking I liked her, we wouldn't have known she'd stumbled onto our little setup."

"Maybe so, maybe so," Randolph admitted grudgingly. "And I bet you didn't mind the fringe benefits."

Billy laughed, and it was no longer a pleasant sound to Jennifer's ears. "Well . . ." His voice trailed off suggestively.

Ohhh! If only she could get her hands around his neck . . . Ken! What must he be thinking? She was half-afraid to look at him. She felt her cheeks flush with humiliation, then she felt Ken's gentle hand on her cheek. Looking up, she saw a tender smile on his face and his eyes seemed to be telegraphing a silent "I understand."

"It's still a good thing you planted those albums in her desk. We don't need her or her information anymore."

"Oh, I did more than that," Billy bragged. "I convinced her that Stanley guy is mixed up in a robbery ring."

"Ha!" Randolph grunted in surprise. "Good old straight-arrow Kenny a crook. How did you manage that?"

"Brains, Len," he said smugly. "Your trouble is you don't appreciate how clever your partner is." Jennifer and Ken exchanged looks and Ken shook his head in disgust. "How much longer are we going to use this place, Len?" Billy asked. "This old warehouse gets on my nerves."

"The new place will be ready in a couple of days. We'll leave everything here until then. I've been checking on Stanley and he's not due back from California for another week, so stop worrying. We're safe here."

Jennifer listened to the two thieves congratulate one another. She hoped they'd leave soon. She couldn't wait to get to the police. Billy Singleton and Leonard Randolph would rot in jail if she had anything to say about it. Satisfying thoughts of revenge swirled through her head. Suddenly, she felt something brush against her leg. *Aggghhh!* It was a rat! A spasm jerked her leg, sending the creature scurrying off into the shadows. Jennifer sighed in relief and leaned heavily against the stack of metal chutes. Too late, she realized the whole stack was moving, and it toppled over onto the concrete floor with a deafening clang.

Chapter 14

Jennifer peeked out as Billy and Randolph hurried across the room to where she and Ken were. "Come on," Ken hissed at Jennifer, pulling her to her feet. They darted from the cover of the railroad ties.

"Kenny?" Randolph cried in surprise. "Is that you, Stanley?"

Ken's words were low and insistent. "Come on," he told Jennifer, urging her toward the far end of the icehouse.

"Where?" Jennifer gasped, stumbling in her sandals as she tried to keep up with him.

"Come on," he repeated, going even faster. How she wished she were wearing jeans and sneakers instead of office clothes!

They ran across an open space between machinery long enough for Billy to see them and yell, "Hey, he's got Jennifer with him!"

They heard Randolph cursing. "So Stanley made the mistake of bringing another friend out here to explore," he said.

"How did that dumb kid figure this out?" Billy was almost whining.

"Shut up," ordered Randolph. "It doesn't matter. Kenny got one friend killed here . . . now we're going to take care of him and his snoopy girlfriend, too! Those two are the only ones who know anything!"

Ken led Jennifer hastily over to a wooden staircase set into the thick wall of the storage room. "Up," he commanded. "It's our only chance."

Jennifer gazed upward. A narrow, rotting staircase rose straight up from the floor and was lost in the dark corners of the ceiling high above. And she wasn't dressed for climbing. "Where does it go?" she gulped as she paused at the bottom, staring nervously into the half light.

"To the ceiling," Ken hissed. "There's no other place to go."

"But didn't Tom Gallagher . . . ?" Jennifer started to protest.

Her sentence faded away and her heart leaped into her mouth when she heard Billy scream, "There they are—at the stairs!"

She protested no more, but climbed frantically upward into the darkness, tripping on loose steps and filling her hands with splinters from the unsteady railing. Ken was right behind her, breathing hard.

As she reached the third floor, Jennifer felt a brace give under her arm and felt herself slipping over the side of the stairs into space. But Ken grabbed her and yanked her back. She scrambled onward in the darkness, afraid to look down now because they were nearing the ceiling. And that was seven stories high.

"I hope it's still there," she heard Ken whisper, out of breath.

"What?" asked Jennifer, pausing on the top landing and hanging on for dear life.

"The elevator!" Ken said, panting as he looked down into the gloomy storage room.

Jennifer peered over the side, too, trying to make out the moving shapes of Billy and Randolph below. "An elevator?" she said, relieved. "That's wonderful!"

"How much do you weigh?" Ken said quickly.

Flabbergasted by such a question at that moment, Jennifer gave him a look and said, "A hundred and five. Why?"

"Damn," Ken muttered. "Not enough."

"What in the world are you talking about?" she said, confused and still slightly out of breath. "You're worrying about my figure at a time like this?"

"Shhh!" he snapped, waving a hand at her. "I think they're climbing up."

"What are we going to do?" Jennifer hissed back. "We're trapped!"

"I knew they'd come up," Ken said. "In fact, I counted on it."

"For heaven's sake, why?"

"Randolph is planning to push us off, make our deaths look accidental."

"Deaths!" she gasped.

"When they come up, we'll use the elevator . . . if it still works."

"Why don't we just go use it now?" Jennifer protested.

"Can't," he said.

"Hey!" A shout rose from the stairway. "You might as well come down! There's no way out of here!" It was Billy.

"That's what you think," Ken taunted him. "We're leaving right now!" Then they heard steps again, climbing upward. "Come on," Ken whispered, and pulled her along the wall.

"Where?" Jennifer squealed.

"There's a catwalk along the wall. Be careful."

Jennifer squinted into the darkness. The catwalk consisted of three or four warped two-by-fours running along the wall near the ceiling. She gingerly put a foot onto it and held herself flat against the wall. *Don't look down,* she told herself. Ken was right behind her.

Jennifer started inching along, leaning flat against the wall when, suddenly, there *wasn't* any wall! "Ken!" she screamed as she fell.

But it was a short fall, because there was a small platform behind the wall. With a thump, Jennifer crashed against something and grabbed on for dear life. A rope! In a moment, Ken was beside her.

"Good going," he told her. "You've found it."

"I found what?" she said, her voice shaking with fear.

"The elevator! You're holding on to the cable."

Jennifer allowed her eyes to adjust to the terrifying darkness that engulfed her. Gradually, she made out the frayed cable she was gripping like a vise. Looking down, she saw she was standing on a metal slab about the size of a boy's sled.

"This is the *elevator!"* She was stunned. "Who used it, midgets?"

"It was for lowering blocks of ice when they were stacked to the ceiling," Ken explained. "The only trouble is, it's a gravity elevator. It only goes down when there are three hundred pounds on it. And I don't weigh one ninety-five."

No wonder he'd wanted to know her weight. "What are we going to do?" she whispered, trying to peek out of the elevator to see if anyone was moving down the catwalk.

"We need more weight," he said.

"Somebody's coming," she whispered. "I think it's Billy."

"Quiet," Ken said.

In a moment, they could hear Billy's labored breathing as he edged closer. He was holding an old board threateningly, as if to hit the first moving thing he saw. "Rotten damn splinters," he muttered. He was only inches away.

If the same thing happened to Billy that happened to her, Jennifer suddenly realized, he would tumble onto the elevator with them!

Almost the moment she realized it, Billy came

147

crashing between them onto the little elevator, hitting his head on the cable. Frightened, he dropped the board and grabbed hold of the elevator cable with a shriek.

"There's the rest of our weight," she heard Ken cry.

And then they found out that the gravity elevator still worked. With Billy's weight added, the elevator suddenly started falling down the shaft at a terrifying speed. Jennifer thought she was going to faint!

But scared as she was, Billy was more terrified, having no idea what had happened! "Ahhh . . . help! Lenny!" he shrieked. And then Ken's fist crashed into Billy's face.

It took only seconds for the gravity elevator to race downward to the bottom of the shaft, where it clanged against the floor with a violent crash. The flat slab suddenly tilted when it hit the bottom of the shaft, and she and Ken were thrown off roughly. Billy, still clutching the cable, stayed on the elevator. Without three hundred pounds on it, the elevator immediately began to rise toward the ceiling again, taking Billy with it.

Dazed, totally disoriented, Jennifer sat up and looked around in confusion. She was in the corridor around the storage room, next to the conveyor belt with the iron teeth sticking up. She had come down just like a block of ice! "Ken!" she cried groggily. She could hear Leonard Randolph's heavy footsteps pounding down the wooden staircase inside the storage room.

"I'm here, Jenny," Ken said from behind her, "but I twisted my ankle when we were thrown off the elevator. Are you all right?"

"Come on," she cried, ignoring his question. "We've got to get out of here."

Moving as fast as Ken's ankle would allow, stumbling over old machinery, they made it to the outer door and into the afternoon light. "We need the police," Jennifer told Ken urgently.

"Run," he gasped. "Get to the car and use the CB radio . . ."

"But will you be safe here?"

"Just run," Ken insisted.

And Jennifer did, all the way back to the car, Ken limping as quickly as he could behind her. Staring at the CB dial, Jennifer puzzled over how to get a police frequency. Finally, she just started tuning in, trying to get anyone at all. "Hello?" she said loudly into the radio microphone. "This is Jennifer Taggert! We need police at the Stanley icehouse on Miller Pond!"

Static and bleeps popped from the radio. "Repeat please."

"Hello . . . police? We are being assaulted at the Stanley icehouse on Miller Pond."

"Ten four," a voice said. "Okay . . . stand by."

Jennifer ducked down in the front seat as Ken reached the car. He was just in time, because a few seconds later, a figure came hurtling out of the icehouse. It was Leonard Randolph. He ran to a parked van, jumped in, and raced down the gravel road.

Jennifer waited, listening for the sound of the police sirens.

Jennifer remembered the thrill of anticipation she used to feel when she walked into the *Springfield Times* in the mornings, tossing a wave at Danny the guard. But this was the first time she ever felt it while dashing out of the paper and down the steps. Ken's car was at the curb. He waved at her out the window and called out eagerly, "Jennifer!" She ran to the car and jumped in. Ken pulled away from the curb, glancing at her at the same time in impatient expectation. "Well?" he asked.

Jennifer hesitated a moment, and then, quivering with excitement, she spread open the front page of the *Times* on her lap. And there on the front page was her story, her first published article, complete with the most magical words in the English language: "By Jennifer Taggert." Her first story and her first by-line!

"Let me see," Ken cried, pulling the car over to the curb and snatching the paper away.

"Our pictures, too!" Jennifer shouted happily.

"Young Reporter and Track Star Smash Record Piracy Ring," Ken read out loud.

"I didn't really write everything that's there," Jennifer confessed. "A rewrite man helped me. But they insisted on putting only my name on it. I didn't fight them on that point," she laughed.

The article took up two columns of the *Times* front page, and it told the whole story. The Springfield police had converged on the icehouse like the Seventh

Cavalry, dragging back with them a thoroughly cowed Leonard Randolph, who had been caught before he got a mile away.

All the rest was there, too—how Billy and Randolph had stolen tape decks and VCRs around Springfield and set up their operation in the abandoned icehouse; how Billy filched the records; how a duplicate file key had been made that night when Randolph stole Jennifer's purse at the Cave. Her spotting Randolph with the purse had almost ruined their plans.

The story didn't mention that Jennifer had nearly been fired, or that when the mystery was finally unraveled, a distraught and tearful Kathleen Owens asked her forgiveness. Not even Ken knew that she and Jennifer had had a private talk. "Being around you has made me so lonesome for Sally," Kathleen confessed. "I'm going to call her tonight. Maybe we can become closer."

"I'm sure you can," Jennifer had reassured her. "I'll bet Sally needs you just as much as you need her."

After they devoured the story, Ken started the car again and drove to Due's for a thick, crusty sausage-and-onion pizza banquet. At the restaurant, Ken looked at Jennifer across the checkered tablecloth and reached over to hold her hands.

"Jennifer Taggert, ace reporter." He smiled, then said, "There's one more part of this story."

"What?"

"We have to drive to get there," he teased.

"Where?"

151

"What would you say to Silver Point?"

Oh, no, she thought. *Not there.*

"Jenny, is something wrong?"

Jennifer took a deep breath to calm herself. "Nothing's wrong, Ken, nothing at all," she said, giving him a glowing smile. "I've got a better idea. Let's go to Alaska!"